SEEDS OF THE YEW

HAROLD BELL

ST. PETERSBURG PRESS

Published by St. Petersburg Press

St. Petersburg, FL

www.stpetersburgpress.com

Design and composition by St. Petersburg Press and Isa Crosta

Cover design by Amy J Cianci and Isa Crosta

Paperback ISBN: 978-1-964239-03-3

eBook ISBN: 978-1-964239-04-0

First Edition

❧ Created with Vellum

TABLE OF CONTENTS

A Quick Note

Hey all, Harold here. I wanted to take a page and acknowledge the experience I had writing my first ever book, ***Under the Yew***, thirty years in the making. Much credit is due to my best friend, Nancy, who typed, edited, and dealt with the process of bringing the manuscript to life. And to Fred, who lay patiently by my side while I talked to myself and tossed wadded up pieces of paper about.

Special thanks to the dozen or so friends and acquaintances who read the manuscript and provided feedback, particularly Donna, Colleen, Becks and Davo, who professed a need to see 'what happens next?' to the Greenbank gang.

Seeds of the Yew picks up the story some years down the line, the narrative driven by what was happening in the world at the time, and the ever-changing dynamic playing out by the big yew in Mossley Hill. Hope you enjoy!

Seeds of the Yew

Cast of Characters

The Greenbank Gang

The Carters – Lucas, Daniela, Jacob, Poppy, and Otter
Cyril Barcant and Colleen Baumann
The McTimons - Kevin, Cheryl, Ian, Seamus, Cyrus
The Ardavans - Abbas, Robin, Gabriel
The Pines - Benjamin, Faith and Barky
The Ardavans - Bashir, Penelope, Rose, Caspar, and Isaac
Neff Boler

The Elders

Michael and Allison Barcant
Eugene and Louise Pine
Ender and Anne Linares
Hassan and Aleah Ardavan
Bus and Mary Carter
Ray and Roisin Mason
Clive Mason

The Electibles

Geoff Higgins, Paul Pilnick, George Pearson, Mike Pinder

The Dovey - Gillian, Emma, Colin, April

The Baltic Fleet - James Doohan, Sarah, May, June

The Echo - John Pugh, Judith 'Moneypenny' Baker

The Kin
Astrid Linares, Cye Ardavan, Catherine Barcant
John and Sylvia Quinn
George and Rose Stillwell

The storyteller makes no choice
Soon you will not hear his voice
His job is to shed light, and not to master

***

Robert Hunter

TEMPEST

Chapter 1

Monday, 1 January

The New Year's onset found Lucas Carter under the yew tree in Greenbank Park. It was cold, only two or three degrees Celsius, but the air was still and dry. He pulled one of the three chairs from under the old card table and sat it up against the trunk of the tree, facing east. The rising sun's glow, alive in the canopy, had silhouetted the neighborhood skyline, the only movement in the form of wood smoke issuing from brick chimneys.

This was Luke's favorite time of day, and he was invigorated by the half hour stroll he'd taken, escorted by Otter and Barky, who were both down on their haunches, relaxed, but still alert, assessing the movements made by whoever or whatever through the park during the night. Their steam breath mingled with tufts of Yorkshire fog grass rising from the ground cover of cocksfoot and perennial rye.

One would suppose it easy to turn reflective on the first day of a new year, and Luke succumbed as his thoughts turned inward. It was under this very tree, ten years ago to the day, that he openly declared love and loyalty to his fellow band of emigrees, and to the city of Liverpool. It hadn't been easy, it still wasn't, but steady progress had been made, sometimes in steps, sometimes in leaps, and sometimes backwards, but neither he nor his friends had any regrets. They were truly happy here, in this city of immigrants on the banks of the Mersey.

Ten years, a third of his life, spent in one place. The previous two thirds had been played out in eight states and three foreign countries. He was a proud American but a citizen of the world, fluent in four languages. A teacher by trade, Lucas taught language to young teenagers at the nearby Quarry Bank Comprehensive School. Adolescence was a challenge, everything seemed so dramatic at that age. Luke's language skills at times were secondary to his ability to counsel and comfort.

On the job training is what it was, Luke had two of his own now. His wife, the former Daniela Linares, was Venezuelan-American. They met during their senior year in high school in Judibana, a small oil camp town on the country's north coast. Luke was in boarding school up in Florida, Dani home-schooled. Over the Christmas, Easter, and beginning of summer breaks they became close friends and, along with Luke's roommate in St. Petersburg, Benjamin Pine, decided to come to England after graduation.

Why England? Cyril Barcant, that's why. Cy was Luke's oldest friend; they'd met in the early sixties in Port of Spain. Their fathers worked together, Bus Carter hiring Michael Barcant to run the crew on Trinidad's first sewage treatment and disposal plant. Their families became neighbors and trusted friends and remained in touch when the Carters moved on. Young Cyril became a footballing phenom, landing a tryout with Everton Football Club of Liverpool in the country's top division.

So, the quartet made their way across the pond and spent the summer looking for, well, themselves, for lack of a better word. What they found was the end of the rainbow, and Abbas Ardavan.

Abbas was from Tehran, Luke's mid-sixties stop between Trinidad and Venezuela, one of a handful of locals that went to the Tehran American School. His mother ran the art department at the campus compound in the heart of the city. His eldest brother, Bashir, had come to Liverpool years ago, attained a teaching position, and started a family. Abbas followed that fateful summer of '69, enrolling at the University of Liverpool and joining the Merseyside Youth Orchestra as first chair flute.

A big slice of serendipity was served up in early June of that same year. Abbas was making his way through a crowded Cooper's Food Hall in the City Centre when a young fellow stood up from his table, smiled, and spoke to him. It was Lucas. From that moment on the five of them were inseparable. Bashir's wife, Penelope, eventually dubbed them the 'Fab Five.'

So, the gang furthered their education, found work in their chosen careers, and carved out a nice life for themselves here in the leafy south Liverpool suburbs.

Luke eyed the five row-home house across the road. A few lights were on despite the fact that it was early morning on a holiday. Kids and dogs, they'll keep you on a routine.

The north end of the structure was Cyril's house. Dani and Luke lived there with he and Colleen, Cy's girlfriend. Next door was the McTimons family: Kevin, Cheryl, and their sons Ian, Seamus, and Cyrus. Ian was in the states, getting his wanderlust on. The middle unit belonged to Abbas and his wife Robin and their son Gabriel. The Pines lived there as well. Ben married Faith in an amazing double ceremony along with Faith's mother Roisin and Ray Mason. Neff Boler, now retired at age seventy-four, lived between Abbas and Bashir. Bashir and Penny lived at the south end with their children Rose and Caspar.

It was quite a collection of characters. Ben's boss at the Echo, John Pugh, referred to them as 'The United Nations of Mossley Hill.'

Three dogs completed the group portrait. Isaac ran the crew, all fourteen pounds of him. Littermates Otter and Barky, English Otterhounds, were his trusted sergeants at arms. The three of them were in charge of security, a job they took seriously.

It was a largely communal existence that arose easily through their strong feelings for each other. They had keys to the others' homes and vehicles, and were trusted with their children and pets. They also supported each other's businesses and careers, and could confide in one another or lean on them for advice.

Despite all the positives in their lives, Luke had reason to feel a bit of unease. The world, as usual, was experiencing its typical ills and hardships, trouble spots around the planet popping up in a seemingly random pattern. He knew this wasn't the case, though. Conflict and chaos were always a result of some root cause, some set of circumstance and occurrence, random or conceived, and finally brought to bear. Luke felt things coming to a head, both at home and abroad, things that had to be sorted. He tried to anticipate when and where fate might rear its ugly head, but that was useless. Better to prepare for the eventuality of it. Besides, Luke didn't really believe in fate. He knew his problems would arise from the machinations of men, and their folly. He did believe in karma, and that, from time to time, even karma needed a nudge.

Otter and Barky suddenly stood and wagged a silent excitement as the front door to the home on the left opened. Dani watched as the bundled young figure walked to the road, looked both ways, and turned back to her for permission. Then he scurried across to and under the posted entry way and bolted towards the yew, juking Barky and Otter and leaping into his father's arms.

"Da come! Mum's making pancakes!"

Chapter 2
Wednesday, 17 January

Time will bring the fire and flame
as surely as it brought the rain

Geopolitical events around the globe can bring about a mixed bag of results. Boundaries redrawn, alliances formed or dissolved, and conflicts, at the negotiating table or on the field of battle, all decided by the few in power. And the general citizenry, the rank and file? Well, they just have to deal with it, whatever the outcome.

Not so in revolution. For one sovereign nation to rise up from within and see its people slaughter each other is to witness abject tragedy.

In Iran the situation smoldered for decades but had ignited in the past fifteen months. There were two factions, the Shah and the Ayatollah. The fact that the two could not achieve a peaceful coexistence meant that distaste and distrust had turned to hate. The hardline religious clerics were prophesizing fire and brimstone by way of Sharia law while the Shah was just as extreme in his use of available force, particularly SAVAK, his own secret police. This left no room for moderates seeking a society where both could thrive.

Things just kept getting more violent. Strikes, protests, demonstrations, assassinations; it was a downward spiral. Martial law was imposed. That just made matters worse. Prisons filled up while the body count rose exponentially.

Abbas and Bashir's parents, Hassan and Aleah Ardavan, learned that the Shah was preparing to leave the country. They put Cye, their other son, on a plane for England the next day. He arrived on Merseyside, haggard and shaken, nearly two weeks ago. Ben, who was a photojournalist for the Liverpool Echo, said the Shah and the Empress boarded a plane yesterday headed for Cairo. Shahpour Bakhtiar of the National Front had been appointed Prime Minister. He was virtually ignored.

Hassan and Cye's architectural firm almost exclusively designed buildings for the government. Their contacts within left no doubt about what was to come. They transferred ownership of the firm to the government, for about half of what it was worth. Better than nothing. The Ardavans also sold their house, the new owner agreeing to lease it to them through the summer. Finally, they transferred the bulk of their assets to Barkley's Bank in London.

What they didn't properly plan for was leaving the country themselves. That's what had Cye so upset. His folks had been threatened, and targeted. Hassan's relationship with the ruling class by itself was reason enough and Aleah's long tenure at the Tehran American School was particularly damning. Any attempt to leave the country now would result in immediate incarceration.

Luke, Ben, and Abbas were with Bashir at his house. Penny was tidying up in the kitchen after dinner. Rose and Caspar were in front of the telly, Cye keeping an eye on them.

"It's maddening not to be able to do anything," Bashir moaned.

"They should've come with Cye," Abbas said.

"I imagine they didn't realize the danger at the time," Luke offered. "Things started happening fast. I'll bet there's not much in the way of reliable news available to them by now."

"I've got an idea," said Ben. "All four of you speak Farsi. Take turns coming with me to work every morning. We'll check out all the news posts coming over the wire. Maybe we can monitor when the airport will be open for either commercial flights or possible humanitarian airlifts."

"I wonder if they could drive across the border. Surely things are too chaotic to watch all the roads," Bashir pondered. "Anyway, it's a great idea, Ben. Surely an opportunity will arise."

"Enshallah," sighed Abbas.

Ben's offer gave Luke a spark of an idea. He knew of one entity in particular that surely must be planning an exit strategy from Iran. If so, it would take something special to include the Ardavans in these plans. Something or someone. A real fixer.

CHAPTER 3
SUNDAY, 21 JANUARY

Once in a while you get shown the light
in the strangest of places if you look at it right

'To the children, our light to the future' was part of a toast Neff Boler proposed at Christmas some years back. Neff was quite the orator when he chose, and his bon mots and words of wisdom wasn't just flowery speech, they had proven to be heed worthy and sometimes prophetic.

The Greenbank gang, distracted and somewhat distraught at current events in the Middle East, found solace and hope in the younger members of their clan. A clan that had grown measurably in the last five years.

Poppy Anne Carter, now ten weeks old, was the newest bundle of joy, born on Remembrance Day, England's time for honoring those that served. She was precious by all accounts, with her dad's light hair and her mom's wry smile. Her big brother, Jacob Neff, was three and a half, an organic wind-up toy with an immense vocabulary. The only problem was no one knew what language he was speaking. In between was Abbas and Robin's son, Gabriel Revaz Ardavan, just over two and a half years old. Gabe was something else. Mobile, ever smiling, and a willing eater and nap taker. He was a strikingly gorgeous little boy, with his father's olive complexion and his mother's auburn hair and blue-grey eyes. It was preordained that he would become a concert cellist and marry Poppy at the age of twenty-four.

Rose and Caspar Ardavan were next oldest. Bashir and Penny's kids were the measuring stick for life on Greenbank Road; Rosie was just a baby when the Fab Five moved to Liverpool. Next month the two would turn ten and seven respectively.

That left the McTimons boys. Kevin and Cheryl were convinced their sons received more of an education from all the expats sharing the row house than any school could teach them. Their neighbors had inspired the lads with the places they'd come from and the experiences they'd had. All three had been in awe of Cyril when they first moved in. Cy was Everton's newest star signing, the boys huge Toffees fans. Since then, Bashir and Luke taught them math and French, Abbas turned Ian into a flutist, Dani encouraged in Cyrus a desire to care for animals, and Shea had earned himself an apprentice pro contract with Everton.

At this rate the children would outnumber the adults before long. Neither Ben and Faith, who were married, and Cy and Colleen, who were still living in sin, had kids, but still, for Pete's sake, someone needed to figure out the cause of all this prodigal fertility.

Thankfully, the Greenbank Coalition was a communal one, a support system forged with love and caring. Cheryl and Neff coordinated daycare, assuring each day's 'orphans' would be looked after. Penny, who worked part-time, was first alternate.

This morning had been a nice, peaceful respite from the hustle and bustle. Those who could slept in, a welcome change. It was very cold outside and a bit raw, hot drinks by the fire the cure. Only the McTimons and Faith were required to answer the call of duty, Faith at the pharmacy and the McTimons up at the family fish and chips shop. It was only open from eleven till five, but Kevin always gave his employees Sundays off.

Cyril had ten days off from training, so he and Colleen, now Colly to most, went to Florida to see her family and enjoy some warm weather.

The rest planned a late afternoon together at the Carter's, Abbas and Robin making a pot of stew and Penny bringing bread and salad. The children, along with the dogs, would provide the entertainment.

Neff showed up last and was mobbed by the youngsters. He was their sage, their Santa, their secret-keeper. And they were indeed his brightest light, bright enough to lead them all.

CHAPTER 4
MONDAY, 22 JANUARY

Travel the days of freedom
Roads leading everywhere
Come with me now, and show how you care

Dusk was settling in on Florida's gulf coast, a slight breeze carrying the scents of jasmine and citrus through the Pine's home on Lake Pasadena. Eugene and Louise were talking with Cyril and Colleen out on the lanai while Ian and Astrid prepared a tray of after dinner drinks. Logistics were being ironed out regarding tomorrow's trip back to England, Cy had to report to training on Thursday and Colly needed to get back to the pharmacy.

It had been a wonderful week, Colly introducing Cy to her family up in Clearwater and catching up with the Pines and their 'kids.'

Astrid, Dani's younger sister, had been living in St. Pete and studying marine biology and oceanography at the University of South Florida's satellite campus just south of downtown. She had finished four years and was now working towards her master's degree. Ian, after one year at the University of Liverpool, had come to the States last July.

Straightaway, he landed a chair in the Florida Gulf Coast Symphony, a needed boon to help with expenses, along with the Pine's hospitality. He also enrolled in some basic classes at St. Pete Junior College, less than half a mile away.

Gene wrapped up a two-term stint as mayor last year, yielding to Sandy Friedman after a refreshingly civil election campaign. At fifty-five he wasn't quite ready to grab his fishing pole, so he hung out a shingle on a small office on Mirror Lake and revived his law practice. Louise served as needed, complimenting his career as she did when he was in the state department. They loved having Ian and Astrid living with them and keeping in touch with the Greenbank gang and their extended families.

"I've pretty much exhausted all my remaining contacts trying to get the skinny on Iran," Gene reported. "There's been assurance of plans to evacuate any and all Americans possible, but no word on aid to any targeted Iranian nationals."

"You'd think they would be glad to let anyone leave that opposed them," said Astrid.

"Well, they do want to get rid of them, but I think they want to bury them, not exile them," Cyril said.

"Their own people," Ian sighed.

"I pray for Aleah and Hassan," Louise interjected. "Thankfully, Cye is with his brothers. Those three must be beside themselves."

"We have to stay positive, and do what we can," Gene advised. "Keep alert, work our contacts. If anything breaks, find a way to get word to them."

The rest of the evening was spent in a more cheerful manner, talk of kids and school, football, and music, catching each other up, and hopeful plans for the future. Astrid had gotten an internship at the Mote Marine Laboratory, a much-esteemed research and educational facility an hour south in Sarasota. They had just moved to their new home on City Island and were also in the process of adding an aquarium to the complex.

Ian had thrown himself into his work at the symphony. They loved his chops, artistic expression, and Scouse personality. He responded with dedication and commitment, determined to become independent of means and repay both the symphony's trust and the support of his friends and family.

He and Astrid had become close, spending most of their free time together. They went to the beach, sought out the local music scene, and supported the area's football club, the Tampa Bay Rowdies. They liked the league, a mix of young Americans and foreign veterans playing out the end of their careers and retiring in the States. Ian gave Cy a jersey to take home to Cyrus.

An early flight meant early to bed. Hugs and kisses exchanged, thanks given, promises made, and hope for salvation in the near future agreed on.

Enshallah.

CHAPTER 5
SATURDAY, 10 FEBRUARY

If our times, they are troubled times,
show us the way, tell us what to do

The past couple of weeks had been maddening. Frustration at the lack of movement, and even the lack of information coming out of Iran saw the gang's spirits sag. They did what they could, continuing to monitor the news outlets and remaining in contact with the U.S. Consulate locally for any new developments. The Ardavan brothers spent time at the Islamic center up in Toxteth. There they found some countrymen, recent arrivals, but they could only attest to what they had experienced; they had no real news to give hope with respect to anyone left behind.

They had managed, with Neff's help, to get the immigration process for Cye started, and to collect information on how to do the same for his parents, should they manage to escape.

Thankfully, they got a boost yesterday, a big piece of news by way of Eugene Pine. Gene fully grasped the danger Hassan and Aleah were in, and he knew that his government was aware of the same peril their own citizens faced, and that action had to be taken soon. This shit could and would go south in a hurry.

He flew to Washington and took a cab directly to a nondescript office complex in Arlington. There he climbed the bureaucratic ladder until someone spoke plainly to him. He learned that there had been a lot happening behind the scenes, and that the imminent new regime in Iran had been convinced that the revolution would not be televised, and that the lot of them would be entering paradise early should American bodies start to pile up.

The result of these mostly one-way negotiations was that there would be a mass evacuation from Tehran in the middle of the month. There had been flights out of the country, but they were sporadic, and privately funded and operated. Some had found their way out down south in the city of Abadan, close to the independent Kingdom of Bahrain, off the coast of Saudi Arabia, both still friendly to the United States.

This, however, was to be a U.S.-led mission, sanctioned by the Ayotollah. Gene's contacts were sympathetic to his plight but had no control over the passenger manifest, particularly with respect to Iranian nationals.

This airlift was to be kept secret, despite its approval. Gene sent a message to the ambassador's residence in London, his old stomping ground, and had it relayed by courier to the Echo offices in Liverpool, attention Benjamin Pine.

Last night, Ben, Luke, and the Ardavans had huddled up, discussing how this could possibly work. Luke was strangely quiet, hearing all the ideas and sussing it out. When he spoke, he was resolute.

"There is only one way, guys." And then he outlined his plan.

"You're kidding me!"

"What!"

"Lucas!"

"The height of foolishness!"

He paused, "Think about it, it could work! I tell you what, let's meet after dinner and put it to the rest, give us a chance to sort it."

Two and half hours later the whole clan was in the park, the kids bundled up, playing with the dogs in the meadow while the adults gathered under the yew. Lucas and Daniela were the last to arrive, the baby in Luke's arms. Dani was pale, her eyes puffy.

Much debate ensued over 'The Plan.' Mostly, Luke was getting castigated, his loved ones confused, angry, and somewhat in disbelief. In his mind though, progress was being made. At least the nuts and bolts of the idea were being discussed.

Cyril, who had been mum the whole time, came to a conclusion. He knew Lucas Carter better than anyone, including probably Dani. Luke's instincts were solid; this guy had a way about him, streetwise and savvy. He also could deliver up a real dose of reality to most anyone that needed it. But he needed confidence to make this thing happen, and the backing of his tribe. His heart ached for Dani; she needed some reassurance.

"All right, my brother, I now see the method to your madness. This plan will work, and you are de only one can make it true. Satan lives there now, Lucas. Deliver our friends from this hell they are in."

He embraced Luke, Dani, and Poppy together as the rest closed in. Enshallah.

Chapter 6

Saturday, 10 February

Can you picture what we'll be,
so limitless and free
Desperately in need of some stranger's hand,
in a desperate land

Alone figure shuffled through the mob, chaos all around him. His destination was still a hundred yards away; getting there was like running a gauntlet. But he kept his nerve, walking slowly, unobtrusively, head down.

Physically he didn't stand out, wearing traditional clothes, baggy pants, plain shirt buttoned at the collar, and a vest with a light jacket. He was clean-shaven, had cut his hair short, and was thankful for the chilly weather and the ushanka, the hat he wore, made of lamb's wool. He had the ear flaps down, hiding the blonde fuzz on his sideburns and the back of his neck.

Those around him were mostly young, all were male, and their fervor fueled the din that enveloped the whole scene. Their passion was not totally unchecked; however, they remained on the south side of the wide avenue, obeying the cordon placed in the middle. The north side of the avenue, plus the broad sidewalk and particularly the centrally located gates to the property beyond, were occupied by the U.S. Marines in full combat uniform.

Lucas Carter made his way to the front of the crowd, chanting right along and waving his fists. He stood there, steeling himself, eyeing the crew at the gate. Then he opened his jacket, unbuttoned his vest, and strode at pace towards the other side. When he reached the halfway point, he felt like the loneliest son of a bitch in the whole world. Then, still in stride, he slowly raised his right hand, took off his hat, and raised both arms into the air, his left hand brandishing his U.S. passport.

Four Marines were striding toward him, weapons aimed at his chest. He locked eyes with the one with the most stripes and flashed his trademark sly grin.

"I'm from Kentucky, sarge, let me in!"

"On your knees, son." They took his hat and passport and searched him. "They must raise 'em crazy over in the bluegrass."

The mob was incensed. Bottles and rocks followed them to the sidewalk. Luke officially requested asylum and was led through the gates.

Two of the detail escorted Luke to the east end of the building, a long, low, two-story structure surrounded by a few acres of open and wooded greenspace, interrupted solely by tarmac behind the embassy on the north side. This east side featured extra security and resembled some sort of processing area. He was interviewed briefly in a small room by a taciturn man, non-uniformed and very terse.

"What brings you here today, Mr. Carter?"

"I'm seeking a safe way out of the country for myself and two friends."

"Where do you live?"

"In England, sir, Liverpool to be specific."

"I mean here, in Iran."

"Nowhere, sir. I just arrived this morning."

The guy stared at him, blankly, for a long time. Lucas stayed mum.

"You flew in just so you could fly right back out?"

"Yes sir. It's because of my friends. They need secure passage from their home to the embassy, or the airport."

"What are their names?"

"Hassan and Aleah Ardavan."

"They're locals?" he asked incredulously.

"Yes sir." He wasn't giving more than he had to. He knew this guy had no authority, he needed to get further up the chain of command.

"I can't authorize this."

"I'm not surprised. Get me someone who can."

Now the guy was pissed. "I should just show you the gate!"

Luke eyed him coolly, "By yourself? Listen, I would not take this risk unnecessarily; these people have been associated with our presence here for a long time. Right now it's a risk for them to even leave their home. We are their only hope!"

The guy stewed for a bit, trying to maintain. Then he stood. "Wait here, I'll be right back."

No you won't, Luke thought. And yes, I'll wait, I'm fucking locked in. He sat back, closed his eyes, and tried to decompress. That scene out in the street had rattled him.

He almost didn't get off the ground to begin with. The plane wouldn't leave until it was confirmed the Mehrabad Airport would be open when it got there. Luckily, it arrived just before dawn, Luke wanted things as quiet and sleepy as possible.

He came as prepared as possible as well. Dani cut his hair, and Cye supplied his outfit. Bashir gave him two wads of cash; he'd exchanged pounds for rials. One was all small bills, for expenses. The other, Bashir said, was for 'baksheesh,' which means a tip, or the amount you would give a beggar on the street. They had gotten a chuckle out of that; this baksheesh was for bribes, hopefully not needed.

At the airport Luke was hoping for a rental, but there was none to be had. He approached four different cab drivers before he found one he felt he could trust. Even then he didn't say he was going to the embassy, opting to direct the driver to a nearby park he was familiar with.

Before he left, he gave a list of four names for Ben to try to track down, either through the Echo or Eugene's state department contacts. The gang was trying to think of anything and everything to gain an edge.

After nearly an hour the second suit came in. This one was a little more off the top rack.

"Let me get this straight; you flew in literally this morning so you could fly back out asap, with two Iranian nationals, no less."

"Correct."

"You've got a set of brass balls on you kid! Do you know what the Ayatollah's thugs will do if they catch us shuttling their people out of the country?"

"Sir, I beg your pardon, but just how much juice do you have here? I mean, do you have the authority to okay this request should I give you just cause?"

"Not personally, but I have the ear of the Ambassador."

The man was curious. It was time for Luke to make his case.

"Hassan Ardavan has spent the bulk of his career designing buildings for the Shah's government. This includes two of the prisons built to detain those people out in the street. They're not letting him out of the country. And his wife, Aleah, she has taught at the Tehran American School, affiliated with this embassy, for nineteen out of the twenty-four years of its existence. Did you have kids who went there? Ask them, ask anyone with any experience at the school. She is beloved. And time is running out, she needs to be a part of that airlift that's being planned."

"What airlift? There's no airlift. Planes leave here willy-nilly with whoever we can put on them. And the locals check everyone out before boarding."

"Don't dick me around! I know it's a hush-hush operation. I also know it's an Ayatollah sanctioned operation. And he knows the shit will hit the fan should anything untoward happen. Look, I left here in '68. Ask Armin Meyer, the former Ambassador. Or Tom Johnson and Bob Hileman, the old superintendent and principal. They all knew Aleah. Sir, these people are pariahs because of us. We hyped the good publicity of a shared partnership here. We wrote articles about how these locals helped us assimilate into their culture. We put their pictures in our yearbooks. Now they're wanted posters. We can't turn our backs on them now."

Luke's plea, and in particular the inside info he possessed, had stunned the guy.

"You're putting me in a bad spot, you know."

"We're all in the shit now, sir. Don't take it upon yourself, run it up the flagpole. Someone will salute."

He afforded himself a grin. "You're determined, aren't you?"

"I am. And I'm not a piece of paper you can shuffle from the inbox to the outbox."

"Wait here."

"Come on man, this is a jail! Let me go to the head, get something to eat."

He hesitated. "All right, confine yourself to the cafeteria though. I can't have you wandering about, starting international incidents. Come on, I'll show you."

"I know where it is. I've been here a dozen times, at least."

"I'm still escorting you!"

An hour and a half later, Luke felt much better. Twenty minutes in the bathroom, followed by a cheeseburger, fries, and a Coke. He was basking in the sunlight streaming through the window next to his table overlooking a patio.

He had just finished talking to a young state department attaché. Apparently, Luke's arrival had created a buzz; his bold move at the gate and subsequent story had some believing he was a spook trying to smuggle assets out of the country. He couldn't blame them for being paranoid, not knowing what to expect next. The guy also updated him on the latest development in country. Over the last two weeks the revolution, the actual takeover, had taken place. The eleventh was declared the Islamic Revolution Victory Day. It was critical times right now; the various opposition groups were acting independently, doling out justice as they saw fit. It would take time for the new regime to bring things under control.

Now a uniform was walking towards his table, steely eyes searching him out. Luke rose. This guy had birds on his shoulders. Now we're talking.

"You Carter?"

"Yes, Colonel. Lucas Carter." They shook hands.

"Lee Holland, let's have a conversation." They both sat down.

"You undertook great risk to put yourself in a bad situation, son."

"Yes sir. I did not see any other solution. To not make my plea in person, I feel would be fruitless."

"How so?"

"I could lay out all the information, make my case and probably the only ones to see it would be the two 'gentlemen' I spoke with earlier here. They didn't even introduce themselves."

"Officious little twits. I see your point. But still, you've really laid it all on the line. You close to these people?"

"Very much so, known them for fifteen years."

"Do they have a place to go?"

"Absolutely. All three of their sons and their three grandchildren are my neighbors. Uncle Sam won't have to spend a penny."

"Well then, I won't keep you in suspense any longer. We've checked you out, you're solid. Regardless, it appears you're well connected. On the civilian side, the Ambassador had me on the carpet, instructing me to extend aid to the Ardavans. This was right after getting off the horn with my commanding officer, who had said the same exact thing in much more colorful terms."

"Sorry for that, Colonel."

"I'm used to it. And now I'm curious as hell. How do you know Major General Harvey Jablonski?"

"I used to date his daughter Alice."

His jaw literally dropped. "And how would you characterize your relationship with young Miss Jablonski?"

"Very respectful, sir."

"Copy that," he said, after he stopped laughing.

"Ole Jabo ran the show around here in the sixties. He's retired now. They found him in Killeen Texas."

"A great man, the General. He and I had some good conversations, mostly one-sided."

"I've also been instructed to help facilitate the Ardavans arrival on site to be processed, along with yourself, onto a bus to travel to the airport for evac."

"That's wonderful news sir. When?"

"This Saturday. Early. Do you know their present whereabouts?"

"They're at home, in my old neighborhood. If the embassy can loan me a vehicle, I can have them here whenever you need us."

"Damn boy, you do have cojones! I'm giving you a vehicle, but my personal driver will take you, and pick you up at 0400 hours Saturday morning. You can trust him. He's former SAVAK, a very capable man."

"Thank you, Colonel. I owe you an immeasurable debt of gratitude."

"You bet your ass. Now, is there anything else?"

"One thing only." Luke produced a piece of paper with Gene Pine's contact info. "You can send a message to this man through your state department liaison. Tell him to let my family know I'm in country and safe."

"Will do. Is this your inside source?"

Luke hesitated, "Yes sir. Please don't burn him."

"Not a chance. I like putting one over on the suits around here."

"Copy that sir."

"Oh, and Carter."

"Sir?"

"You're just a schoolteacher, right?"

"A damn good one."

"Fortune favors the brave."

The driver's name was Asghar, a hard looking man indeed. He was good for some small talk, appreciative that Luke spoke Farsi, but not much for real information. He was also well-armed. The roads required his full concentration; they had to detour from time to time to avoid demonstrations, rubble, or burning vehicles.

Lucas had always embraced the surreal in the past, part of the wonder of life. These scenes, however, chilled him to the bone. Cyril was right, Satan resided here now. They passed an abandoned construction site, equipment scattered about. There were three cranes lined up, booms extended high into the air. Bodies hung from all three, a harbinger of times to come. He shuddered and turned his head.

Up in the neighborhood, he explained where the Ardavans lived, but had Asghar drop him off a block early, at the corner. He walked west to almost the end of the block, where loomed the steel and stone fencing that was the eastern boundary of the Shah's Winter Palace. A small cul-de-sac led him up to the gate leading into their yard. No one saw him as he went around front and knocked on the door.

Hassan answered, cautiously, as Luke removed his hat and flashed a broad grin. He shouted to Aleah, opened the door, and motioned him hurriedly inside.

"Luke, what the hell!"

"Hi Hassan, I hear the rates are cheap during a revolution." They embraced. Aleah appeared from the hall to the mud room and kitchen and buried her face into Luke's chest, already sobbing.

"Aleah look, Allah has sent us a miracle!"

"Even better," she tearfully burst out. "He has sent us Lucas!"

Chapter 7
Wednesday, 14 February

Women waiting at the harbour,
silent stand around
Weather storms another day,
for men the sea had found

They don't always come home. That thought kept entering Ben's mind, and the personal impact he felt from it, given the current circumstances, weighed on him heavily.

He was on his way down to the office, and he had opted for the bus. The extra time, some fresh air, and not having to drive helped him think, and compartmentalize. He liked his thoughts to be organized, all in their proper little cubby holes, waiting to be called on.

They don't always come home. This really didn't refer to Lucas, though the thought remained with him. It was a phrase he heard his boss, John Pugh, the Echo's editor, use when describing the state of recent events the paper covered. The IRA had maintained its campaign into England. Four weeks ago, bombs exploded almost simultaneously in Liverpool, Manchester, Coventry, Southampton, and Brighton, where there were fatalities. Then there was an apparently lone bad guy, dubbed the 'Yorkshire Ripper,' who had managed at least eight or nine grisly murders thus far. Yes, sadly, they don't always come home.

He tried to let his brain change the subject. Not everything was gloom and doom at the moment.

Today was Valentine's Day, which was also little Rosie's birthday. He made a mental note to get two cards, one present, and some flowers. Also, he was making progress on his book, a project that would allow him to channel his inner author.

And although they'd heard nothing out of Iran yet, the source of everyone's angst, Ben and his father had some success with Luke's hit list.

The Fisk family had been located in Arizona, south of Tucson. Colonel Fisk, now retired, knew Aleah by way of his wife, Donna. Mrs. Fisk and Ben had a nice chat about the old days. Her son, Tom, was in a band called 'The Mimics' with Luke in the eighth grade, and the Colonel and Tom had taken Luke and Jeff Carpenter skiing at Abali in the Alborz mountains north of town. Donna Fisk was also the secretary to the principal of the school, Robert Hileman. They were shocked but not really surprised at Luke's present situation and promised to use their contacts to get a message to the embassy.

An even better result came out of locating one Major General Harvey Jablonski, also now retired, and living in Killeen, Texas.

"Luke Carter? Yes, I know him. What's he done now?" the general asked. Gene explained the situation.

"The teacher, I don't know her, or at least can't remember. I'll check with the family. I can vouch for Luke, though. Good character. He was one of the few that learned the language. That kid was squirrelly though."

After some more chitchat, Jablonski said he would go over to nearby Fort Hood and get a message to his people in Tehran.

Ben got off the bus two blocks from the Post and Echo Building, not far from the waterfront. The Mersey was shrouded in fog, with only the tops of the three Graces rising above the mist. He'd barely made it inside the front door when Moneypenny, aka Judith Baker, John's secretary, assailed him with a telegram. Judith was aware of the goings-on and was eager to hear the news. Ben opened it. His embrace lifted her right off the ground.

"He made it, he's at the Embassy!"

"Thank God! Ring up Daniela, give that poor girl some relief!"

CHAPTER 8
SATURDAY, 17 FEBRUARY

Let's meet as friends
The flower of Islam
The fruit of Abraham

Asghar was out front at the appointed time. It was still dark out, a chilly breeze filtering down through the foothills. He opened the trunk as the trio came down the front walk and quietly loaded up.

They were limited to one suitcase and one carry-on each. Lucas only needed the carry-on, and he advised the Ardavans to do the same, leaving the three bigger pieces for valuables and keepsakes. Luke was also packing a sidearm, a very formidable Colt M 1911 forty-five automatic. It was Hassan's weapon, given to him by an American construction worker years ago; he said he'd never fired it. Luke stripped it down, cleaned and oiled it, and loaded it with hollow points. He'd decided beforehand not to tell the driver; better to keep all options open.

Asghar opted for a more eastern route to town, eschewing the main roads for the suburbs. The trip took longer, nearly an hour, but proved to be uneventful.

Last night they had eaten simply. Labu and ash, roasted beets and porridge, and the last of a loaf of bread. The conversation was excited but nervous. You had to pity the two, having to leave their work, their home, and their country. At least they'd be with their family, if this proved to be a successful operation.

They arrived at the embassy's west gate and were waved through and directed to a parking area where Asghar dropped them off. Luke thanked him, then asked if he had a desire to leave Iran himself. He smirked, thanked Luke, and demurred. One day, maybe; there was more work to be done here first. He also told Luke not to push his luck, his wry smile met in kind.

The rising sun, combined with local atmospheric conditions, created a golden glow on the ground, lighting up the faces of all those gathered on the tarmac behind the embassy. There were hundreds. Men, women, children, even pets, all gravitating towards the twelve buses, lined up and facing east. Luke and the Ardavans joined the queue.

Caravans were certainly a normal way of life in this part of the world. The one that exited the eastern side of the embassy grounds that morning was one that defied logic. Luke noticed that there wasn't a big security detail attached to the group, a couple of Marines per bus and one vehicle each at the front and back of the procession seemed thin. Once out on the street, however, the convoy was led by members of the Ayatollah's own volunteer army. Such was the tacit threat that the U.S. military imposed.

The twelve buses contained a total of eight hundred people. Everyone had been processed overnight, exchanging their passports for receipts used for boarding, where the trade was reversed. Many had slept in the cafeteria. Everyone was tired and haggard but hopeful.

The trip took about a half hour and was tense but uneventful. They did pass by Tehran University, where about a hundred young men stood behind sandbags, heavily armed. The scene was draped with banners bearing Islamic slogans and the symbol of the Hammer and Sickle. These kids, in Luke's mind, were mightily confused. He caught the eye of one guy who waved goodbye to him. He flashed him a peace sign in response.

The airport was closed but busy. There were already about four hundred British and French citizens present, waiting on an evac from the Royal Air Force and Air France, respectively.

Hassan and Aleah looked for a spot to settle in and wait while Luke went to the bathroom. Inside the stall, he unloaded the sidearm and put everything in a small case. Then, he went to find Colonel Holland.

"Ah, Mr. Carter, you made it."

"Morning Colonel. Yes, thanks to Asghar."

"And where are your charges?"

"Cooling their heels, sir. Would you like to meet them?"

"Absolutely. I'd like to see what all the fuss is about."

"First, let me give you this, Colonel. I can't take it on the plane, or at least wouldn't want to." Luke handed him the case.

"Let me guess."

"It's not loaded, sir."

He sighed.

Hassan and Aleah had found a reasonably quiet corner. They rose as the two approached.

"Mr. and Mrs. Ardavan, I presume?"

Hassan extended his hand. "I am Hassan, sir. This is my wife, Aleah."

"Please to meet you, sir." Then he took Aleah's hand in both of his. "And you too, ma'am. You need not worry now, you're in the hands of the United States Army. You will leave here today safely. And I'm very sorry all this is happening to your country."

"Thank you, Colonel. You have surely saved us."

"No, ma'am. That would be young Carter here. There is, apparently, a method to his madness."

"We think he's pretty special."

"Please don't encourage him." They laughed. It felt good.

"Here's the plan, folks. There will be two Pan Am 747s to leave first, followed by another 747 and a C-141 military transport. I'm putting you on that last bird. Less comfort, but better security. Fighter pilots think twice before locking onto the stars and stripes. Not that I'm expecting trouble, mind you."

"Copy, sir. I'd be willing to assist in any way in the interim. I can speak French as well as Farsi."

He smiled, in spite of himself. "At ease, 007."

"Aye, sir."

Time passed. The British left around noon. The French were distraught, their flight was cancelled. Everyone was still hopeful but on edge. Kids and dogs roamed about while others slept or talked amongst each other.

Aleah found a few former students and colleagues to catch up with; the school had been closed since last year. Hassan was glad to see her time being occupied in a more positive manner, she'd been so sad lately. Luke found people to talk to as well. He was curious to hear if some of his friends from the old days were still around. Some people actually sought him out. All the embassy personnel were aware of his escapades the other day and word had spread. It seemed that the pique and puzzlement he had caused had turned to curiosity and wonder.

The Americans amassed were of various backgrounds. Besides all non-essential embassy staff, there were employees and their families working for Lockheed, Bell Helicopter, General Telephone, and the companies supporting the oil industry, among others. Over forty thousand U.S. citizens were in Iran when the trouble started, compared to only ten thousand when Luke lived there. Most were already gone.

The boarding commenced mid-afternoon. Lee Holland was a picture of professionalism and organization. Both Pan Am flights took off, followed a short time later by the non-descript 747 and the C-141. In a no doubt rare moment of sentimentality, the Colonel complimented and congratulated Lucas and told him to keep his head below the parapets.

Not surprisingly, spirited applause and raucous cheering accompanied take off, along with a massive sense of relief.

It was announced that the destination was Rhein-Main Air Base at Frankfurt, more than halfway home. On arrival they were processed out and driven into town. Luke had learned about a nice hotel to splurge on, the Steigenberger Hof, and they checked in at dusk. Luke immediately phoned Dani, who had to put Colleen on because she was too choked up to speak after learning he was okay.

A long, hot shower followed by schnitzel, spaetzle, and beer, followed by nine hours of sleep and another long, hot shower.

Next stop Liverpool.

Chapter 9
Monday, 19 February

Breathe deep as you enter sleep
Feel secure, it's all around you

Given all that had happened, Ben thought it wise to ease the Ardavans into their new environment, purely from an emotional point of view. Aleah and Hassan had been on Merseyside for visits off and on for the last twelve or thirteen years, but this time, however, was obviously different. He tried to imagine how they felt, like refugees probably, which is exactly what they were. Of course, their family was here now. They would, in time, feel secure and once again find a sense of belonging. But to watch your own country burn from within must leave a scar on your very soul.

The gang had three estate cars now. Yes, Bashir's self-proclaimed 'Greenbank Coalition,' as he had dubbed the rowhouse collective, was slowly becoming the empire he'd envisioned. Along with Ben's Morris Traveller and Cyril's Hillman Husky, Luke and Abbas had bought a slightly used Vauxhall Victor FE. It was bitchin'.

Abbas and Bashir drove the Morris and the Vauxhall to the Liverpool Lime Street Station, the welcoming committee consisting of only the Ardavans and Carters. Only, meaning all eleven of them: three wives, three brothers, and five children.

They parked off Bolton Street and walked two blocks to the station's southwest entrance, a massive arch of steel and glass. The arrivals board displayed the track number, the train due to arrive any minute.

Out on the platform they waited, scanning the incoming passengers. Robin saw them first, getting off the third car. Rose led the charge, followed by Caspar, Jacob, and Gabriel, his little legs pumping furiously.

It was too much for Aleah, overcome with all she'd been through combined with the emotion that now overtook her. She dropped her bag and sunk to her knees as her grandchildren rushed into her arms. Her sons embraced their father.

"Da!" Jake shouted. "You rode a train!"

"You betcha!" he answered, holding his little boy close. "You miss me?"

"You betcha!"

Dani had Poppy Anne in her arms, tears running down her cheeks. He grinned.

She shook her head. "Mi niño." They held each other for a long time.

The two blubbering masses of humanity eventually broke up and headed outside, the blue sky confirming a fresh new outlook. Robin and Gabe rode home with the Carters, mostly to even out the load as well as to allow the Tehranis the moment. Uncertainties loomed for the Ardavans; at least now they were together. Bring it on.

Hassan and Luke had a long talk on the plane that morning, hashing over the last week and discussing future plans in general. Hassan was concerned over living arrangements in the short term.

"Not to worry," Luke assured him. "Neff has moved his bedroom to his downstairs study and is using the small bedroom upstairs for storage," he explained. "You have the rest of the upstairs. No, don't protest, the man is excited. Says a woman's touch is just the ticket. The guy is sincere, Hassan, and smart. Now he'll get more home cooking."

They also broached the subject of Luke's actions back on the first day he arrived in Tehran. He had said it could not have worked out any better. He flew in, got a ride to the embassy, and got a ride up to the neighborhood. All true, basically. Aleah and Hassan learned differently, from an old colleague at the airport when they left. This man had spoken to one of the Marines that challenged Luke in the street outside the gate.

"Are you kidding me, Lucas?"

"Please, let's keep this between the three of us. Dani will clip my wings."

They parked at the curb at the center of the rowhouse. Home at last. Everyone got out and the guys grabbed the bags. No one was coming out to greet them. They heard a dog bark from behind and turned to look. There they were, everyone but Colly and Kevin, under the yew.

There were no tears at this reunion. A flock of starlings, chattering in the canopy, scattered at the sudden joyful noise on the ground. Feel secure, it's all around you.

Chapter 10
Tuesday, 6 March

So let's skip the news boy (I'll go make that tea)
Blood on the rooftops (too much for me)

After a couple of weeks the Ardavans had found their footing, and rediscovered their smiles, surrounded by family and friends. The first few days saw Hassan and Aleah taking long walks in nearby parks, savoring the peace and beauty of late winter in the northwest of England. Gradually, they immersed themselves in the clan's day to day routine, helping around the house and with the children's morning up and at 'ems. The rest of the gang were cheered by the brightened outlook, confident that the coming spring would relegate sadness to the sidelines.

Lucas took one extra day off and then went back to work. Man, a lot went down in seven days. Some of his students found him a bit distracted the rest of that week. He still had some decompressing to do.

Daniela returned to her post at the Edge Hill Animal Hospital, the baby old enough now to be left with others. There would always be volunteers; Poppy was the clan's little sweetie. Dani loved her job and the rest of the staff and was dedicated to her work.

The Ardavan brothers got their groove back on, Bashir the head-teacher at the local primary school, and Abbas, along with Robin, musicians at the Royal Liverpool Philharmonic. Even Cye had found that his architectural experience was impressing the local firms. Employment, however, was still illusive due to the worsening economy and lack of projects going forward.

Cyril was back at it, the short break in January a distant memory. Everton was in good form; the boys were in the midst of a solid season, currently in fifth place.

The McTimons owned their own business, a fish and chips restaurant in Wavertree. Kevin and Cheryl's clientele were loyal, the food was really good, but overall receipts reflected hard times locally.

Everyone was excited about the new business venture undertaken by some of the gang. The Mason brothers, Ray and Clive, bought an existing pharmacy on Smithdown Road just south of the Penny Lane roundabout. The guys had been working stiffs, doing the nine to five for nearly forty years, and decided to get into business for themselves. To be honest, they didn't know squat about the industry, but that was where Faith and Colleen came in.

Faith had been a licensed pharmacist for over four years. Colleen followed in her footsteps, completing her postgrad work and one year on the job apprenticeship last fall. Both were now members of the Royal Pharmaceutical Society.

There was much discussion beforehand, and a lot of legwork and research undertaken. In the end, all parties involved were up for the project and eager to get to work.

The name on the new sign out front read Erins Pharmacy, Erin being both Colleen and Faith's middle name. They would be filling the prescriptions, now dispensing drugs together instead of pints, as they did a half mile away at Dovedale Towers. Faith's mum, Roisin, would keep the books and help out in the store, which was stocked with all the various and sundry items you would find at such a place.

April Walker was recruited from the Dovey as well. She would run the cash register. Gillian, the manager at Dovedale Towers, carped about how the Greenbank Gang had stolen all her help. Inwardly, however, she was happy to see her girls progress and thrive.

Ray and Clive would look after inventory, maintenance, and the like while Seamus McTimons would come in for an odd job now and then.

The past ten years had seen the Masons get sucked into the Greenbank Coalition's universe, but they seemed to be enjoying the ride. They had met the group at the Abbey, a popular pre-match watering hole a block from Goodison Park. Cyril had become their favorite footballer, and his friends from far flung lands had taken to the Evertonians. Now they were family, Ray marrying Roisin alongside Ben and Faith.

Barky, Ben and Faith's dog, rounded out the new store's staff. He was in charge of security.

TRIAL

CHAPTER 11
FRIDAY, 9 MARCH

Miles and miles I have roamed,
looking for that home sweet home

Ben held the print up and studied it. He was standing by the window in his office, preferring the natural light to the fluorescent bulbs in the overhead fixture. He was pleased with his choice of shots, looking east at the Merseyside Ferry, passenger laden, still about sixty yards from docking at Pier Head.

It had been cloudy that day, and raw, the wind blowing in off the Irish Sea. He was in a police patrol boat, there for an interview, and took the opportunity to snap off a few pics.

It was the best of the lot, the Royal Iris, the first diesel-powered ferry; a slight lean to starboard under stiff winds, waves crashing the bow, frozen in time.

The photo, and accompanying text, were to be the first chapter in Ben's book, 'Missives from Merseyside.' He thought it appropriate since the first sight that many people encountered arriving at the city by vessel was the docks.

He returned to his desk and set the print aside, turning to the text itself. It was based on an interview he'd had with Roisin, his mother-in-law. His plan was to let a different person tell their own story of what the subject of each photograph meant to them:

My name is Roisin Ryan, and for me the ferry is a symbol of hope. Hope for a new start, a new beginning.

My daughter, Faith, and I come from Ireland. County Clare, south of Galway. It's a grand place, so green and peaceful. But times were hard, and daily life seemed a struggle even before my Jim took ill. When he passed, we were utterly bereft.

We sold everything we had. It wasn't a lot, but it got us two tickets on the ferry from Dublin for the day's journey to Liverpool. My brother Tom had left the farm at sixteen to come to England. He helped us at first; we felt overwhelmed.

I wanted Faith to go to university, and we managed it, her working as a barmaid and keeping up with her studies while I got a job in the Wirral at Birkenhead as a bookkeeper.

For this I got to ride the ferry every day! It's how I learned all about Liverpool, from the people, going about their normal routine. Faith would always ask about who I spoke to today and what happened on the ferry today. There was always a story to tell. People are very friendly here.

Did you know that I actually met Gerry Marsden on the ferry itself? Gobsmacked I was. Such a nice boy, always smiling. Naturally, people gathered round, we all ended up singing 'Ferry Cross the Mersey!'

We've been here nearly ten years now. It's our home. And we've grown our family, there's a clan here we're part of.

I don't have to take the ferry anymore, but from time to time, I still find reason to do so anyway. It's grand!

So ferry, cross the Mersey,
And always take me there,
The place I love.

CHAPTER 12
TUESDAY, 13 MARCH

Well they say time loves a hero, but only time will tell

Cyril's history with Everton Football Club was basically a love story. It was his first and only club as a professional. They'd given him a look as a favor for an old friend of then manager Harry Catterick, and he'd responded by being named to the senior squad right away and remaining loyal to the club for nearly ten years now.

A health scare had relegated Catterick to the sidelines, and his replacement, Billy Bingham, a former player, had some success but had been moved on two years ago.

The new manager, Gordon Lee, was a bright student of the game and appreciated players who would always put a shift in. Cy both liked and respected his gaffer. He liked his skipper too. Mick Lyons had been one of his two best mates at the club and had been the team captain since '75.

When Lee was hired, he assessed the squad's makeup, declaring that lots of people like stars and flare on a football team. He had always thought that stars are found only in the sky and that flare only belonged at the bottom of your pants. 'Have all the showy lads you like. I'll take eleven Mick Lyons any day.'

He held Cyril in high regard also, saying he was the first name on the team sheet, as well as describing him as 'molded of steel with a silk scarf.'

Cy was on his fourth contract with the Toffees, only once had there been any issue with the terms. The memory always brought a smile to his face, it was back in seventy-five. Three years prior he was given a modest raise after his initial contract was up. That was fine with him; he appreciated all the other little ways they had brought him along. But he had become a stellar top-flight performer and had captained Trinidad and Tobago on an improbable run at the '74 World Cup in Germany. Now considered probably the best holding midfielder on the planet, he had been surprised and a touch tender at his home club's anticipated lack of commitment to him.

Footballers didn't have agents like movie stars and the like; typically, your parents were present at the first meeting with the board. After that, you were given what they deemed fit, or you may be sold to another club, or simply dropped. 'Surplus to our needs,' they would claim.

Cyril realized it was, after all, a business, so he took the same approach. He requested a meeting with the owner, the chairman, and the board. And he took Lucas with him, as his 'representative.'

Luke had the reputation of being worldly and streetwise, a guy who could get things done. He certainly was that guy last month in Iran. Cy still needed to get to the bottom of that whole ordeal, he knew his old pal was holding back.

Anyway, Cyril and the 'Fixer' went to the meeting looking like they'd just left Saville Row and calmly, quietly laid out the way it ought to be. Luke had a briefcase with correspondence from some of the top destinations in Europe. Letterhead bearing the crests of Real Madrid, Ajax. AC Milan, and Bayern Munich. He casually displayed them. No big deal, he said, just a distraction. Then he spoke that 'Lucas speak,' friendly and soothing, but with an undercurrent of finality. The suits didn't know what hit them. Cy was so happy with the outcome that last year when his contract was up he simply walked in and told them he'd sign for the same exact terms. They gave him a slight bump anyway. The chairman, John Moores, said it was for not having to deal with 'that Carter chap.'

Cy suspended his reverie, bringing full attention to the moment. He was in the away side's changing room at Anfield. It was Derby Day.

A derby was a match pitting rivals against each other, usually from the same town or very nearby. Some of the more famous derbies were North London, the Tyneside, and Manchester, but none were bigger than the Merseyside Derby. Everton and Liverpool had been at it since the late eighteen hundreds. Their stadiums, Goodison Park and Anfield, were separated by less than a mile of grass in Stanley Park.

Much had been at stake in recent years. Liverpool's fortunes had been turned around by manager Bill Shankly, and his successor, fellow boot room coach Bob Paisley, had hit the ground running. Liverpool were defending champions and at the top of the table. And in second place? Everton.

Cy didn't hate Liverpool. He knew some of their lads, and the city was happy when either team won silverware. For the Scousers on the team however, it was a massive game. It made no difference to Cyril; he wanted to beat 'em all, from Brighton to Newcastle.

Neff was the only Reds fan at Greenbank, even though he was trying to recruit Hassan, Aleah, and Cye, all of whom he brought to this evening's match. They joined over fifty-two thousand other Liverpool supporters, now creating a din that literally reverberated through the walls of the stadium complex.

The teams took the field to the strains of 'You'll Never Walk Alone,' penned by Rogers and Hammerstein and adapted by Gerry and the Pacemakers, becoming the most iconic anthem in world football.

The Ardavans had not seen Cyril play in person, their only prior exposure being two of Trinidad and Tobago's games in the World Cup on television. They were amazed. The atmosphere alone was so electric, so compelling. And Cy, he was a gladiator, skillful and physically dominant. It was so contrary to the kind, accommodating young man they had grown to care so much for.

The game ended in a draw, one all. Kenny Dalglish netted for the Reds after fifteen minutes, and Andy King equalized for the Blues fifteen minutes before full time. It was the hour in between that was remarkable. Two clubs at the top of the league duking it out, give and take, leaving everything on the pitch.

It's typical to see a club bring a full squad to any particular match, the bench containing all of its allotted substitutes. When a team has injuries, which is virtually always, those players' slots are taken by some of the better players on the youth team. Everton brought up two of their youngsters for this match. One of them was Seamus McTimons.

The kid was over the moon! He'd earned the call-up, having impressed in training. The club was betting on him to be a full pro before long. Shea was a natural winger, full of dash and dart.

Tradition called for a football team's shirt numbers to be one through eleven, each number signifying the player's position on the pitch. When Cyril signed for Everton, they gave him the number six, the defensive midfield spot. Right from the start, they were that sure of his quality. The fact that Shea was handed the eleven shirt was significant. Cy had helped him along, especially with the off-pitch aspects of being a professional; but Shea had game, already showing some guile to go along with his skills.

The pair showered and changed with the team, exchanging banter with the lads. Then they jumped in Cy's Hillman and drove to Mossley Hill and home, Shea getting a hero's welcome as if he'd scored the winner.

Chapter 13
Thursday, 5 April

One watch by night, one watch by day
If you get confused, listen to the music play

Abbas and Robin got back home just before noon. The spring season for the Royal Liverpool Philharmonic Orchestra was about to get underway, necessitating a lot of rehearsal time. Thankfully, there was no afternoon session scheduled, affording them the rest of the day off to celebrate this, their fourth anniversary. Their plans included spending the afternoon with their son before going out to dinner.

"Baba!" Gabriel called out as he waddled down the front walk of the McTimons', Cheryl watching from the stoop. "Hi Mama!"

"Hello, my gingerbread boy!" she answered as Abbas scooped the toddler up into his arms. "Hey Cheryl, you okay?"

"Never better, luv. Gabe's had his lunch."

"Alright, catch you later."

The house was deserted. Ben and Faith both at work, along with Barky. There was a card with a nice sentiment and a ten-pound note including the message, 'First round's on us!'

Perfect roomies, they were. Ben and Abbas had bonded from the get-go, nearly ten years past now. Embracing the single life for as long as they could, good times were had at the ole bachelor pad, eventually giving way to the charms and wiles of the female persuasion. They never knew what hit them, and didn't care.

Robin and Faith fell right in together as well. They were so different in appearance and background but enjoyed each other's influence and company. And the both of them were determined young professionals, making their way forward.

All four were from different countries. Combined with the rest of the gang the group as a whole thrived on the diversity of its individuals, sharing and caring together.

After a quick bite, Robin and Abbas took Gabe across the street into Greenbank Park for a frolic along with Otter, who'd been hanging out with Neff. Both Otter and Barky, littermates now almost eight years old, were naturally protective of their whole pack, but it seemed they were aware of the younger one's vulnerability in particular. Everyone remembered the time Otter had to snatch young Caspar out of the lake.

So, the two happily cavorted around the park, entertained by Mother Nature and each other while the happy couple strolled behind, holding hands.

Abbas certainly was more at peace now, having his folks safe and sound and coming back to life. Robin had been so worried about he and his brothers, she just couldn't imagine the range of emotions they'd been through, still fearful of what might befall their country.

The latest news was that Iran officially became an Islamic Republic on the first day of April, just four days ago. Strict dress codes, for men and women, were implemented while opposition political parties were outlawed, and some news outlets were shut down. The executions continued.

Robin wanted to go to Iran one day. Abbas spoke so glowingly of Tehran, nestled in the foothills, a crossroads of culture and ancient civilization. She wanted her son to learn about his heritage, Celtic and Persian. She wondered if it would ever happen.

It could all be so confusing at times; best to simplify things when you can. They had everything they needed right here.

"Abbas, my love, how about a jam in the garden with the gang after dinner? I could use some music!"

CHAPTER 14
SUNDAY, 15 APRIL

From the northwest corner of a brand-new crescent moon,
crickets and cicadas sing a rare and different tune

Neff Boler's house never smelled like this before, and he couldn't be more happy about it. A princess had taken up residence within, and each day brought fresh new evidence of her influence.

The new living arrangement really did suit him well. There was a brightness about the place after the initial emotional unease.

Come to think about it, Neff's life on Greenbank had been a series of bright surprises ever since Bashir's brother Abbas and his band of buddies hit town. Their communal approach and lifestyle had been impossible to resist, and he willingly succumbed to their gravitational pull.

Hassan and Aleah felt it as well. They had been liberated and comforted by the clan, now ready to embrace their new lot in life.

Yesterday Aleah had gone down to Adam's Apple and met John and Sylvie Quinn, Robin's parents and owners of the fruit and produce market on Allerton Road. She had a monstrous shopping list, planning to cook for the whole gang. They had a nice chat, the Quinns supplying what they could, then Sylvie taking Aleah to complete her list. She ended up extending an invitation. "Please come, you've been so nice, and helpful!"

Feeding twenty-five people takes a bit of planning, and cooperation. Cyril and Lucas were recruited to set up the garden, tables, bins, firepit, and the like, while Colleen and Daniela helped in the kitchen. It was a nice, clear night, chilly but still. Escorted by Venus, a crescent moon was rising in the southeast.

The faithful filtered in, lured by the aroma of simmering dishes of exotic origin. A menu would have been useless, unpronounceable words of undiscernible inception. No one cared. Bring it on.

The platters were brought out, and Aleah said the magic words, "Noosh-e-jan!"

One of the dishes was a fairly simple pilaf, with jasmine rice and a variety of nuts and dried fruits. The children could load up on this in case they found the other fare too much for their palates.

"This is all such a treat!" exclaimed Penny. "Looks like your sons were just warming us up for this feast with their cooking, Aleah. This is spectacular!"

"I hope you enjoy it, Penny. The drinks are all outside."

Somehow it always seemed that Cyril, Cye, and Cyrus ended up together, now sitting on the edge of the firepit, utensils busy. The Cys Men, as Ben had dubbed them years ago, were much enjoying the meal, Cyril loving the seasonings, similar tasting to Caribbean fare.

Everyone had a couple of ladles full of the stew, a concoction of lamb, tomatoes, and chickpeas called dizi. "Man, I could fill up on this alone," Luke said, tearing off a chunk of thick and crusty barbari bread.

Rose, now ten years old, commanded a table that included her brother Caspar, her cousin Gabriel, and Jacob. A younger version of Penny is what she was, no adult supervision necessary.

Robin and Dani sat together, little Poppy in Robin's arms, cooing at all the activity. "She's precious, Dani, how's her appetite?"

"Constant, it seems. She's starting to wean herself, little by little."

Seamus was sitting at a table with Ben and Abbas, looking confused.

"Mum said to try everything, and so far it's brilliant! This, however, I don't know what to do with it."

"That's dolmeh, Shea. It's rice and beef, with some herbs. It's wrapped in a grape leaf. And yes, it's been soaked and seasoned. You can eat it."

"It looks like an old, soggy, cigar," he replied.

Ben took a bite. "Wow, it's very good! I wasn't sure either, Shea, have a go."

He ended up eating a couple more.

Faith and Colleen were in discussion with Kevin and Cheryl. The subject? Keeping abreast of how to run a small business and stay in the government's good graces. A balancing act, indeed. Apparently, a worsening economy only served to bring about stricter guidelines and more stringent tax rates. Kevin was savvy in such matters, though, promising to get with Roisin to help her with some creative bookkeeping. "Nothing illegal, mind you, just taking all you're entitled to."

The surprise hit of the evening proved to be the fesenjan, browned chicken and toasted walnuts, seasoned, and simmered in a base of pomegranate molasses. Nirvana!

To say that the pups were attentive was an understatement. Isaac, Rosie's Border Terrier, was, as usual, everywhere at once, making himself available. Otter and Barky, massive Otterhounds, politely sat at attention, silent, shaggy behemoths with long, elastic strings of drool, beckoning, pleading, hoping for a handout. This food would overtax their canine digestive systems, Dani warned, only rice and fruit for this pack.

Dessert was in the form of halva, a baked confection made of sesame paste and honey, served with chai tea.

Afterwards some wine was poured, and the adults gathered around the fire pit, immersed in compliments to the chef and general happy chatter.

The kids played hide and seek, the gates between gardens open, as they normally were of late, another sign of the bond that existed amongst them all.

"To our hosts and hostess," Kevin proposed. "Their warmth and charity exceeded only by their wisdom and experience, our path forward."

"Hear hear!"

"Cheers!"

Neff surveyed the scene, illuminated by the flame and the still rising crescent moon. The younger children were by the fire now, close to their kin. This lot would grow up strong and true, he thought, and kind. They all thought of him as their Opa, their parents thankful for his presence. He thought himself most fortunate.

CHAPTER 15
THURSDAY, 19 APRIL

I have got what I once dreamed of
as a child, so long ago

"Full name, please."

"Daniela Elena Linares Carter."

The clerk paused, not willing to try to spell or repeat it, the look on her face a mix of wince and wonder. "What would you like us to call you?"

"Dani Carter."

"Thank God!" They both laughed.

She was in the City Centre, a small office in a large building, paying her dues to become a member of the International Alliance of Women. It was formed after the turn of the century, the male-dominated establishment not paying particular attention. The organization grew and expanded its focus to all issues facing women. Currently, the alliance's president was a Brit; one Olive Bloomer.

Dani received her information packet and was promised that an I.D.

card would arrive by Royal Post within a fortnight. She stepped out into bright sunlight at three in the afternoon, free for the rest of the day.

Her interest in the movement wasn't out of need, she had no real complaints concerning her lot in life, but wanted to show her support of those that did.

In a way, Dani's career ran parallel to the struggle for equality, as exemplified in the Women's Liberation Movement and the efforts to pass the Equal Rights Amendment. She started vet school in the fall of '69, the year after women went on strike at the Dagenham Ford plant. In 1970, as a result, the Equal Pay Act was passed. Also the same year, Sally Alexander and Jo Robinson kickstarted women's lib in England by disrupting the Miss World contest in spectacular fashion.

She did encounter male bias and plenty of attitude at the university, from faculty and students, but she persevered. Since she started practicing in '75, however, such experience was rare. That was down to Julius Pope, who owned Edge Hill Animal Hospital. Jools was a peach. He treated her very well; they'd grown the practice together.

Her girlfriends had their own stories, of course. She knew Faith and Colleen had suffered their share of boorish behavior when they worked at Dovedale Towers, and Robin had spoken to the 'status quo' at the symphony, despite her obvious talent. This attitude had deep roots in society, as well as the workplace. No doubt Penelope and Cheryl could attest to that.

Progress had been made, and it would continue, because now there was unity. Their heels were dug in.

Dani felt a fresh sense of that unity. It was empowering. She made her way to the bus stop for the ride to Mossley Hill.

There were two people at the stop, and they were obviously having a row. A young couple, the man gesticulating wildly at the woman, cowering under the verbal assault.

Suddenly, he slapped her in the face, hard enough to send her to the cobbles. Dani arrived as the bus was pulling up and started to help the sobbing girl to her feet.

"Mind yer own business, bitch!" He grabbed Dani by the left elbow.

"Get your hands off me!" she said icily, looking him straight in the eye. He didn't.

It all happened at once. Dani squared her left foot, stepping back slightly on her right, and drove her fist into the dude's nose. Just like her father taught her, straight from the shoulder, twisting ninety degrees as it landed.

His eyes crossed, watered up, then closed as he fell back on his rump, blood and spittle forming a frothy mask that flowed onto his jacket.

Dani helped the girl on the bus and paid her fare. Asshole tried to stumble aboard in a rage, blocked by the driver, a female driver.

"Take the next one, wanker!"

CHAPTER 16
FRIDAY, 20 APRIL

Let me bring you all things refined:
Galliards and lute songs served in chilling ale

Ben had forgotten which day he took the photograph; it was at least a couple of months ago. He was on Crawford Avenue, about ten yards from where it dead-ended on Penny Lane. Looking almost due east, Dovedale Towers shone brilliantly in the bright sun.

The building was erected with three main sections in the original structure, dominated by the clock tower in the center. Ben's position provided for a straight-on shot, encompassing all the 'gingerbread' adorning the Dovey's façade.

The popular pub, and the gang's go-to spot for a number of occasions, was his choice for Chapter Two in 'Missives from Merseyside.' He'd interviewed Geoff Higgins for the installment. Geoff's family had owned the Dovey until a few years ago; he was well-versed on its history.

Ben sipped a cup of tea and reviewed the text:

. . .

Oy, I'm Geoff Higgins. Hard to know, really, where to start, the Dovey being such a big part of my life for a very long time now.

It was originally named the Grove House, constructed in the 1800s for a wealthy shipbuilder, with a view of the waterfront from the clock tower.

Industrialist Andrew Kurtz was the next tenant, a patron of the arts and apparently quite the pianist. He established what would become a rich musical tradition at the place before eventually donating the house to an orphanage, the Home for Incurable Children.

Then more twists and turns as nearby St. Barnabus Church used the house as its parochial hall, bringing the music back. This brought Paul McCartney here for the first time, singing in the church choir.

What followed is what I like to call the Dovey's 'Golden Age,' tongue in cheek. Now with the name Dovedale Towers, my family became the proprietors, enjoying over ten years at the pub. Good food, ales and some fantastic musicians have been served up, with a bit of history.

Paul, John, and the Quarrymen performed here. Even my band, the Wreckage, originally Ibex, had Freddie Mercury on board for a time. He lived in the flat upstairs.

Then there's The Eclectibles. What started out as open mic night turned into a musical collective that took the city by storm. Abbas Ardavan, a flutist at the Phil, moved into the neighborhood. He and I formed the band, the lineup different at nearly every gig. Brilliant musicians, mind you, Mike Pinder, Aynsley Dunbar, and Robin Quinn, now Abbas' wife, among them.

Hard times financially forced the Dovey's sale. My parents getting too old for the fight. Things are a bit dodgy at the pub at the moment, the economy, no doubt, playing its part. The new owners did retain our manager, Gillian Parry, and they'd be wise to keep her. Gilly's the best!

The Dovey is a Mossley Hill institution, part of its heartbeat. The place has a soul. Come and have a look!

CHAPTER 17
SATURDAY, 28 APRIL

Please, please, listen to me children
You are the ones who will rule the world

Daniela had taken Poppy, swaddled, nothing visible but pink cheeks, down to Neff's house for the day. Aleah was going to watch her instead of Cheryl, who was at the chip shop with Kevin.

"Ah, fereshteye mani!" she cooed. "Good morning, Dani."

"Sobh bekheyr, Aleah. Where's your guys?"

"Neff took Hassan down to the docks; some type of building is taking place."

"You know the old saying, 'you can take the architect out of Iran, but you can't take the architect out of the architect.' Wait, that's not right."

Aleah had a giggle, "I know what you mean."

"Good morning, Aleah. Good morning, Dani." It was Cyrus, coming up the walk.

"Hey, Cy. You ready?"

"Yes, ma'am."

"All right, let's do some healing!"

"You two have a good day."

"Thanks. We'll see you later."

They took the Vauxhall up to Edge Hill to the clinic, Saturday typically being the busiest day of the week.

Cyrus was a great kid, Dani's pet from the get-go. Bright, sensitive, and a fast learner, he also didn't shy away from anything at the practice. He could clean kennels, restrain any type of pet, and he'd observed some surgical procedures. He was there when you needed him and stayed busy when you didn't.

As they were getting things cranked up at the office, Bashir and Cye were boarding a bus headed for Toxteth, Rose and Caspar in tow. They were going to the Masjid Al-Rahama on Mulgrave Street.

It was more than just a mosque, also containing a center for Islamic studies. A good-sized complex, there were spaces for meetings and prayer, instruction and celebration, the crescent moon-topped golden dome dominating its profile.

Penny and Bashir wanted their children to learn about Islam, as well as Christianity, to explore their customs and beliefs, in order to understand the world as a whole a little more clearly. Their religious devotion, should it develop, was their choice. They were also learning some Farsi, Lucas a more than capable tutor.

Both Rose and Caspar were dressed traditionally, Rosie a little princess in her chador. Bashir dreamed of taking his children to Iran one day to experience the climate, the land, and its people. He wondered when, if ever, this would become possible. For now, this day of learning about a part of their heritage would have to suffice.

Abbas and Robin would, one day, introduce Gabriel to his Middle Eastern roots, but, with less than two weeks before his third birthday, there was plenty of time for more mundane pursuits, such as hanging out with his mate Jacob, nearly a year older.

It was big fun riding on the top of the double-decker bus to the City Centre with his dad and Luke, almost like a carnival ride on the narrow, twisty streets. Jacob was in complete agreement, chattering away in his multi-inflected, indecipherable 'Jake speak.'

Luke and Abbas had custody of the toddlers today. They had errands to run, shopping mostly, all taken care of in the morning. Then the boys were introduced to the Liverpool Central Library on William Brown Street. The complex consisted of several grade II listed buildings, the highlight of which was the round Picton Reading Room, a gorgeous piece of design and function. The boys were wowed.

They grabbed some lunch and walked down to Coronation Gardens, between Paradise and South John Streets.

It was a very popular spot with the nine-to-five crowd to take lunch on nice days, a big, open greenspace amid all the hustle and bustle. Housewives would meet during shopping outings for a chat and students would hang around as part of 'the scene.'

Abbas and Luke sat, and people watched as the lads frolicked, running about and chasing gulls. Jake and Gabe were quite the pair, the former's personality and the latter's cutest ever looks too much for the ladies, several pausing to engage the boys, maybe even cop a cuddle.

"Man, Abbas, this is better than bringing puppies!"

"So true, my friend."

A couple of hours later Dani and Cyrus were back in the Victor, headed home. They had opened up the practice in the morning so Jools would lock up at five, with only a couple of more patients scheduled. Thankfully, a hectic morning had settled nicely.

They stopped at the chippy to see how busy it was. Kevin and Cheryl had it under control. Dani got a takeaway for her, Luke, and Colleen. Cyril had a home game, the Toffees hosting Birmingham City.

On the way to Greenbank, Cyrus asked Dani if she would like to hear a poem he'd composed.

"A poem? Yes, I'd love to hear it. Is it for school?"

"No, I just wrote it one day, just sitting at home."

"I'm all ears!"

The boy grew serious and seemed to stare blankly at something in the distance.

"It's called 'At Odds.' This world is so confusing, though I try with all my might. So I put it under my pillow, but it keeps me up at night. Still, I wonder and worry, what it's all about, and if I'll ever sort it out."

Dani was stunned, not sure at first what to say.

"That was very good, Cy!"

"Thank you."

"Deep stuff, bud. Is it something you think about a lot?"

"No, just sometimes."

"There has been a lot of meanness in the world of late. Abbas and his family are sad about their country."

"And in Ireland, there's lots of killings, mostly about God."

"It's more complicated than that, Cy. There's been lots of hate, building up for lots of years. And it's about who makes the rules, and freedom to choose for yourself."

"When will it stop?"

"It's anybody's guess. Listen, don't worry too much about these things. Troubles are all over the world. They get sorted, eventually. It's a brilliant poem, and you are wise beyond your years. Keep alert, and keep asking questions. One day, everyone your age will make the rules. You can fix it."

"Okay. Thanks Dani."

"You're welcome. Now, when we get home, will you go and get Poppy from Aleah and bring her down to me? I'll get this food in the house."

"Really? Yes, I'll be careful!"

"Thanks, pardner!"

She was coming up the front walk, munching on a chip, when Ben and Faith came out of their house, excited postures escorting them her way.

"What's up kids?"

"We are, the three of us!" Ben exclaimed.

"What am I all spiked up about?" Dani asked.

"Not you, luv, the three of us!" Faith said, holding her belly.

Dani literally dropped her takeaway, squealing with delight. Ben rescued the meal while the two hugged it up, tears starting to flow.

Cyril came out the front door on his way to Goodison for the match.

"What's going on?"

"Faith's pregnant," Ben reported.

"That does it. There's something in the water around here!"

Chapter 18
Saturday, 5 May

The men who go from Merseyside
to sail the seven seas,
will hear the call of Everton
come riding on the green

The last day of the English First Division's season was, obviously, one of finality. Forty-two games of blood, sweat, and toil for the players, and nine months of fears, hopes, and dreams for their supporters would culminate in the publishing of the Football Association's archives.

Football in England, and much of Europe, was based on a pyramid system, which meant promotion and relegation. If you were in the bottom three at season's end, you played in the next lower division the next year. If you finished top three, you were promoted. This was huge. It dictated ticket prices, merchandise sales, sponsorships, and player recruitment. Even the local economy was affected.

It sure made for compelling entertainment, with matches at both ends of the table so important. In the first division, you couldn't gain promotion, of course, motivation here was playing in Europe. The top teams from each country's first division qualified for the next year's tournament, known as the European Cup, held during the season on off weeks. A lot of prestige and big money.

A club's finances were key; there was no draft system to obtain players. You either bought them from another club or developed them through your own youth academy.

Everton's dream of the league title had faltered in the last month, but they were still high enough in the table to play in Europe. A loss today would probably end that dream as well.

It was a tough assignment, a road game in north London against Tottenham Hotspurs at White Hart Lane. Kick-off was at three, so the team traveled down the day before.

Cyril was pleased that Seamus was named to the squad. The bus ride, hotel, and hostile atmosphere would test the boy even though he probably wouldn't play. Cy thought this a sign of Gordon's intentions; the gaffer was grooming the kid to be a Blue. It wasn't enough to be able to play the game, you had to be able to live a footballer's life. It's a grind.

The day broke cool and clear, and the lads were boisterous during the team meal. The Toffees would put in a proper shift.

The Lane wasn't the best of grounds overall, but the pitch was a carpet, and the place oozed class, the bronze spurred cock standing watch from on high, just west of the river Lea.

A raucous crowd greeted the players out of the tunnel. Cyril felt something suddenly coarse through him, that familiar call to battle. He grinned widely as derision swept over him, their most vocal supporters baiting him from the Paxton Road end stand. He loved it.

Spurs had a killer trio of players to contend with. Young phenom Glenn Hoddle, a product of their youth system, and newly signed Argentines Ricardo Villa and Osvaldo "Ossie" Ardiles, fresh off from winning last year's World Cup. All three were midfielders, Cy's plate was full.

The match started with about ten minutes of cat-and-mouse, both sides feeling each other out. Spurs then began to probe, first through Hoddle, which Cyril wasn't having, then through the Argentines down the wings, whose crosses center backs Colin Todd and Cy's mate Mick Lyons dealt with.

Everton were being pinned back though; Tottenham were playing mostly in Everton's half.

They committed themselves a bit too much up the pitch. Cy intercepted a pass and pinged it up field in the path of a streaking Andy King. King chipped the ball into the box where it was met by Brian Kidd's diving header. One-nil.

A quiet crowd became recharged at the start of the second half, urging their lads on. Spurs responded with a quick goal on an Ardiles header early on, setting up a pressure-packed finale.

Cyril was the busiest guy on the pitch, followed by his goalie, George Wood. The Toffees were standing firm into the seventy-fifth minute, but Spurs were relentless.

Gordon decided on a sub, the boss needing some speed to keep the opponents honest, make them defend the break. Two minutes later, Seamus McTimons made his senior team debut for Everton Football Club.

Standing on the sideline he looked like a deer in the headlights. Knowing this was not a meaningless appearance, he had to help get the Blues over the line. All nervousness ended two minutes after his introduction when he flattened Glenn Hoddle with a tackle that the referee had no problems with.

And the boy was a threat, being a pest all over the midfield with his pressing, then making runs toward the corner flags when the ball turned over. The kid's energy and commitment buoyed the rest of the side; Wood's goal was not seriously threatened the rest of the match.

It ended in a draw, fourth place in the league and a spot in Europe secured. The whole club went to the away supporters' section to thank their fans, some of the players tossing their shirt to the young Evertonians.

Spurs were lauding their fans as well, the last game of the season at home a special occasion. The players brought their families onto the pitch, along with all the coaches and support staff.

Ossie Ardiles was a class act, doing something Cy would never forget. Knowing what a kid from the streets felt when he made it to the big time, to see an improbable dream come true, the Argentine World Cup winner sought Shea out.

"I'm very happy you did not play the whole game, eleven. You were very good!"

"It's an honor to be on the same pitch as you, sir."

"I can say the same. Can we trade the shirts?"

Shea's grin said it all.

CHAPTER 19
MONDAY, 7 MAY

Too many people sharing party lines
Too many people never sleeping late
Too many people, paying parking fines
Too many hungry people losing weight

Ben's mind was a maelstrom, too much to process at once. He sat in his office, trying to put every item competing for his attention in its own little cubby hole.

Margaret Thatcher, the 'Iron Lady,' had just been elected Prime Minister three days prior. A staunch conservative, she rose through the ranks as a member of Parliament in '59, then she became Secretary of State for Education and Science before defeating her old boss, Edward Heath, to become leader of the Conservative Party. Constituents in labor and liberal dominated areas like Liverpool braced for the worst.

Worrisome issues at the year's onset hadn't resolved themselves. The economy sucked; the Yorkshire Ripper claimed his eleventh victim, nineteen-year-old Josephine Whitaker of Halifax, and the IRA had run amok, its campaign of violence spreading now across international borders. And, Ben would have to check to see which part of the labor force was on strike and which ones were getting laid off this week.

Also, something was constantly at the back of his brain, pushing, probing, trying to come to the fore. What was it? Oh yeah, his wife was pregnant. He smiled, in spite of himself. He was taking off early today. John had told him not to bother at all, but he wanted to come in and get organized for what little he was planning to do this week. He had a piece to turn in, and a couple of rolls of film for the lab.

He also had to make an appointment to interview one Chrissie Mayer over in the Tuebrook area. Chrissie was quite the social advocate, and had started her own neighborhood paper, the Tuebrook Bugle. It focused on local news, drawing the attention of the powers that be to issues such as sanitation and living conditions. The woman was the people's watchdog; calling out even the National Health Service on their communications, citing as an example the government's two hundred-and twenty-nine-word definition of 'bed.'

"Benjamin Pine!" Geez, he nearly fell backwards out of his chair. It was Moneypenny.

"Good morning, Judith. You scared the hell out of me!"

"I'll do worse if you don't go home to Faith. You've only just knocked the poor girl up, now you just carry on sipping your cup of tea!"

"How did you know?"

"From Mick. Cyril told him on the way to London on Saturday and I slept with him last night. And stop grinning like a fool!"

"Sorry, lass, you too much!"

"Well?"

"I'm going, I'm going. I had some things to sort. You won't see me till near the end of the week."

"That's better. And buy her some carnations on the way home. They're for mothers, you know."

"Yes ma'am."

CHAPTER 20
FRIDAY, 11 MAY

Instincts of revelation
Drinking in exaltation
We move around

Cyril pulled himself out of the heavy surf and plopped down on the beach towel next to Colleen.

"I thought you came here to recover and relax?"

"This is relaxing, if I don't drown. These waves are too good to resist."

"They're huge! We never get breaks like this in Florida. Did you learn to body surf in Trinidad?"

"Yeah, at Maracas Bay. Lucas taught me."

"Really? When was this?"

"Early sixties. We were nine, Luke swims like a fish."

They were at the Praia do Norte, North Beach, soaking up the sun, sand, and sultry delights of Portugal's Atlantic Coast. Nazaré was the location, a picturesque fishing village about eighty miles north of Lisbon.

Cy and Colly, in the third of a nine day stay, were loving this sleepy little town, and already establishing a routine. Sleep in, ride bikes or walk the area in the morning, hit the beach in the afternoon, party at night. Their diet consisted, so far, of fresh seafood and port wine.

Their room was in an inn situated centrally in what was originally a village called Sitio. Along with Pederneira, another old settlement further inland, and the Praia neighborhood on the coast, Nazaré became the town's name due to a sixth century legend.

Apparently, a monk brought a wooden statue of the Virgin Mary to a seaside grotto in the cliffs, where a chapel was built to protect it. The statue was from Nazareth, in the Holy Land. The moniker was adapted to the local dialect as Nazaré.

In modern times Nazaré was gaining popularity, bordering on cult status, because of an underwater geological formation known as Nazaré Canyon.

Just offshore, the canyon combined with the ocean to produce some of the world's biggest waves. There were always a few long boarders from places like Hawaii, California, Australia, or Brazil hanging around the waterfront. The elevated, rocky point near the south beach contained a fort, São Miguel Arcanjo, a prime viewing spot for watching the waves, which regularly topped seventy feet, from trough to crest.

Cyril could get used to this. Portugal had a couple of big clubs, Benfica and Porto. He wondered if either needed a six who loved to tackle.

Colly and Cy's bedroom back home was now occupied by Anne and Ender Linares, just arrived from Judibana. Today their granddaughter Poppy turned six months old, the first opportunity for them to be with her. Ender had thought he couldn't be any happier after Jacob was born. Finally, a boy. But he was glued to this little girl, his 'Angelita'. He was with her and Jake right now, under the yew.

Anne, meanwhile, was smoking a joint with Luke, Dani, and Abbas up in the Carter's attic.

"Whoa, no more for me. The only time I smoke is with you hoodlums."

Luke loved his mother-in-law. Dani always said he and her mom had similar personalities. Anne was from Tucson, originally, and had grown up streetwise and independent, a product of a broken home. Her easy-going manner and sharp wit carried well in almost any situation. An expat herself, she was a major force in the encouragement of the gang to emigrate all those years ago.

"Thanks, kids. How about a beer?"

"I can take care of that," offered Abbas. "Robin's cooking for the eight of us tonight, Ben and Faith included. But for now, my folks want you to come to Neff's for a visit. My mom says she's got a surprise for everyone."

"Cool!" Lucas replied. "I'll help with the cervesa, Obs."

Aleah and Hassan hadn't seen the Linares' since Dani and Luke's wedding, Anne now rushing to embrace them both.

"I'm so sorry about what's happening in Iran, and so thankful you are here now, safe!"

"Thank you, Anne, it's great to see you. What do you think about all our kids?" bragged Hassan.

"It's amazing! All they've accomplished is impressive enough. And the togetherness they have, the love they show for each other, is just wonderful."

"Have you heard the latest?" asked Aleah.

"Probably not. Things seem to happen fast around here."

"Faith is with child!"

"Really? Fantastic! How's she doing?"

"So far, so good."

"When's she due?"

"November."

"Wait till I see Ben! Big, gentle Ben. He'll be a good papa!"

"And what's this about a surprise?" Dani prodded. "You've got us very curious just now."

"Just have a look behind you," teased Hassan.

"Wow, kittens!"

Sure enough, there beside the sofa, two little ones in a cage, curiously peering out at all the commotion.

"I'll let them out," Aleah said.

Timid at first, Abbas soon had them chasing a little fluff ball, the cutest things.

"Where did you get them?" Dani, always the vet, asked.

"At a bus stop in Toxteth, two kids had a box full."

"I'll take them to the clinic tomorrow or Sunday and check them out."

"So adorable," Anne said, stroking the one with yellow fur. "Have you named them?"

"Just this morning, we wanted to get a feel for them," said Aleah. "We've decided on Pari and Div."

"Very cool!" Luke declared, knowing what that meant. "Which one's the bad ass?"

"The gray one, Div, a kind of Jinn, or mischievous spirit, according to Persian folklore. Like a genie, but with malevolent intention. Div is male. Pari is female. A Pari is a beautiful, winged spirit, a more benevolent type of Jinn after doing penance for atonement. Jinn are common throughout Islam."

Luke picked up Div. "Sorry, little guy, you've already got a bad rep."

"What about the dogs?" asked Abbas.

"The hounds I'm not worried about," Luke said. "Ben and I have them dialed in. We'll have to watch Isaac, though. That dude's intense."

Chapter 21

My time coming, any day, don't worry 'bout me, no
It's gonna be just like they say, them voices tell me so

Cye Ardavan reflected on the last five months, how fast the time passed, and how it had affected him.

His presence in England, brought about by circumstances beyond his control, seemed like a type of waystation, a temporary purgatory in which his fate would be decided before being shipped off to some place chosen by someone he'd never met.

He couldn't be blamed for a fragile psyche; the past few years had seen his world come apart. The revolution had taken his home, his livelihood, and his country.

Thankfully, he'd come to Greenbank. Cye was a classic middle sibling, the quiet one. He could be quite friendly and engaging, one of the gang, but tended to be the observer, never the first for show and tell. His brothers, and their families, friends, and extended tribe were changing that. He was accepted, cherished, and encouraged to take stock and go again.

Anyone would be lucky to have such a support group. He was offered work, part-time positions mostly. He'd put in some shifts at the pharmacy, but a full-time job in architecture was not in the offing at the moment. His credentials were impressive, his experience vast, but the local firms just weren't hiring due to the economy.

Then, just last week, something broke, something exciting enough to make him show his new-found confidence by moving to yet another country. This morning, he awoke and realized he'd made the decision; he was moving to America.

People thought of Lucas as the 'Fixer;' he'd certainly shown his mettle in the past. Eugene Pine was a fixer before anyone had coined the term; his career in the State Department required it. Gene took retirement hard, parlaying his global skills in tact and diplomacy into the office of the mayor of St. Petersburg. After two terms guiding the city, he still kept his nose in other peoples' business, like helping Luke get Hassan and Aleah out of Iran.

Last week Gene turned his attentions to Cye, resulting in interviews with three prominent local architectural firms. He also started Cye's immigration process, pretty much a formality considering the change in Iran and the States' relationship. And, he and Louise offered Cye a bedroom, very much anxious to get to know him. Cye joked about wondering if the Pines had started filling out adoption papers.

So Ian and Cye were to become roomies. Astrid, however, was moving on, her internship at Mote Marine turning into a full-time position and support for her master's degree studies. She was looking for an apartment in Sarasota; St. Pete was a bit far for a daily commute.

Bashir and Penny celebrated the news at breakfast this morning. They knew Cye was getting antsy. Bashir, in particular, was buoyant. He left for work extolling the ever-evolving power and influence of the Coalition. Cye's new opportunity meant that it was not only growing, but also expanding its reach into the Americas.

CHAPTER 22
FRIDAY, 18 MAY

In another time's forgotten space
your eyes looked from your mother's face
Wildflower seed on the sand and stone,
may the four winds blow you safely home

Café Tabac was a popular place with the crowd from Greenbank, particularly Ben and Abbas. It was at the top of Bold Street, literally a stone's throw from St. Luke's church. Open all day and most of the night, the café morphed from an early morning grab a cup and read the paper place into a soup and sandwich and what have you stopover through the afternoon, then into an evening food and drink see and be seen nightspot.

The clientele was a mixed bag as well. The consistent aspect of Tabac, however, was that the later it got, the more bohemian the mix tended to be.

The café was owned by Rita Lawrence, famous for her vast collection of hats and notorious in her no nonsense running of the establishment. Be as out there as you like but mind your manners.

It was a popular place for Liverpool's creatives, musicians, writers, actors, poets, and those that set their own trends and were not led around by the latest fads and fancies.

The one garnering the most attention at the moment was Gabriel Ardavan, presently being cooed at by a pair of young ladies who reminded Ben of vampires.

"Oh, he's just an angel! What's his name?"

"Gabriel."

"You see? I knew it!"

Faith and Robin were there, the five of them at a corner table with Margi Clarke, an aspiring actress.

"Gabe is one of the most striking children I've ever seen!" she agreed. "The boy will need representation soon."

Margi was a regular at Tabac, referring to it as her 'office.'

"It's the only place around that has a public telephone. My agent rings me up here when something's on."

"What's on your calendar now?" Ben asked.

"Oh, that's right, I haven't seen you in ages. I'm a presenter for 'What's On.' It's an entertainment magazine type of show on the telly."

"That's fantastic!" Faith said. "Congratulations!"

"Thanks, luv. I'm still trying to get into films, it's frustrating at times."

"It's good experience, Margi," offered Robin. "And it puts you out there to be noticed."

"True, that. Any exposure is bound to help."

"Have a look at this lot, Pete!"

It was Jayne Casey and Pete Burns, just arrived.

"'Ello!"

"Introductions?"

Ben spoke up. "I know Mr. Burns. Hey, Pete, hello ma'am, I'm Ben, and this is my wife Faith and our friends Robin and Abbas, and their son Gabriel."

"Jayne Casey, pleased to meet everyone. Pete's mentioned you, Ben. A journo?"

"Uh huh, at the Echo."

"Brilliant!"

Margi spoke up. "Robin and Abbas are members of the Phil."

"That's not all, now I remember," said Pete. "You two are Eclectibles!"

"Yes!" echoed Jayne. "I saw you at the Everyman! So good!"

"Thank you, both. We're going to play another gig in the fall."

"The Eclectibles could sell out a show every week!"

"How's things at the record shop, Pete?" Ben explained to his roomies that Pete worked at Probe Records on Button Street.

"Good. I'm not there as much lately. I'm in a band now, Nightmares in Wax."

"Boss name!" commented Faith. "And you, Jayne?"

"Aye, a musician as well. Our band is Big in Japan."

"I'm sure!" Everyone laughed.

"And what's on here? Are we conducting a union meeting?" It was Rita, smirking mischievously under a monstrous chapeau of chiffon and feathers.

"Ah, the proprietress. No, no, nothing untoward happening here," Margi pleaded.

"Another round?"

"This one's on me," Pete offered.

Abbas spoke up, "Here, you two take our seats, we've got to get ourselves back home."

"You're right, Obs. Faith, Ben?"

"We're coming as well. I think Cyril and Colleen are back from their trip."

"Bring the lad with you again," Rita said. "I'll be needing another cuddle soon from the little darling."

As it turned out, the night was just getting started. All the lights were on at the end house, the north end, and more than a dozen of the gang were there.

"Let's check it out."

The music was on, all the lights were on, and Ben would swear smoke was wafting out of the attic. The kids and dogs were running amok.

"Hey all!"

"Hey guys!" a very tanned Colleen said as she passed out hugs and kisses. "I'm married!"

"Dere's me brothers and sisters!" as Cy joined the love in.

"Cyril, Colly said you're getting married?" asked Robin.

"No, my love. She said we are married. Would you like to kiss the groom?"

Chapter 23

Saturday, 26 May

There's danger on the edge of town
Ride the King's highway

Faith and Seamus were walking up Penny Lane, a light but steady rain dappling their umbrellas, Barky leading the way. They almost always walked to the pharmacy, less than a mile from home.

"Are you sure you need me today?"

"We can always use your help, Shea. Saturdays are busy normally, and there's always chores to be done. We intend to take full advantage of your time this summer, young man."

He smiled. Things were on the up in his world; he was getting on at Quarry Bank, the fall would signal his last year in secondary school, he was earning some extra money, and he seemed firmly in Everton's plans, always his dream.

Erins Pharmacy was in a three-story building on Smithdown just off its intersection with Penny Lane, even with the now famous shelter in the roundabout. The building was erected to fit the curve it occupied, and contained five businesses within, ground floor level with flats upstairs. The pharmacy was on the right, bordering Cronton Road.

Roisin was already present, in the back office preparing a till for the front register. Faith relocked the door, turned on the lights, and went for her lab coat, very fetching to Shea's eye. He toweled off Barky and saw to his water bowl.

They had a cup of tea and chatted until a couple of minutes before eight.

"Okay, then, all hands on deck," Faith announced. "Shea, would you do the honors?"

He went to the front, flipped the sign to open, and unlocked the door.

Two men were waiting to get in. Seamus didn't quite like their look but hey, the shop was open to the public. It takes all kinds, his mum would say.

They no sooner got in the door when one of them, tall and lanky with longish greasy dark hair, turned the sign back over. The other, stout, with curlier dark hair, pulled a knife.

"Let's have a look at the register," he ordered, pointing over to the left at the counter.

"There's nothing in it yet," he lied.

Curly grabbed him by the collar and put the blade to his throat. "You'd better be telling the truth, ya little wonk!" He motioned at the back of the store, on the right.

"There's another register back there. And maybe some other delights, eh?" His grin was disgusting.

The three went to the back, near the entrance to the office. Faith was there, she went pale.

"Good morning, lassie. Aren't you the tall and sexy!"

"Stay behind the counter, Faith."

The punch landed just in front of his ear. He saw stars, the hold on his shirt preventing him from hitting the floor.

"You bastard!" Faith screamed. This brought Roisin out from the back office.

"Alright, missus, stand with the other bitch! Go on now, or you'll get the same!" This from tall and lanky. Roisin's eyes narrowed as she obeyed, furious.

The brief commotion drew the attention of Barky, who was back in the storeroom. He pushed through one of the double-swinging doors and padded down the back aisle towards the source.

He saw them all at once; only Faith and Roisin were facing him, Faith with one open hand slightly upraised.

He stayed but he didn't sit, something had awoken in him. Something primal. His ears went back as his tail went still. He did not make a sound.

"So, ladies, let's ave it," Lanky spewed. "Drugs and money. Quick now, my mate's losing patience with this whelp. I think he's about to be carved up good and proper."

"Fuck you greaseball!"

Faith shouted and raised her fist.

"What's that for? You having a go?" Curly laughed.

Faith smacked her fist into her other hand, open palmed.

The sound Barky made was otherworldly, borne from instinct and duty, fueled by loyalty. You wouldn't think an animal that big could move so fast.

Curly released Shea, who immediately raked his shoe down Lanky's right shin. This was followed by a straight right to his cheek. Then Shea drove the guy straight through a floor display, merchandise flying about. They started wrestling and trading punches.

Curly tried to avoid Barky's rush, but he too was driven into a shelving unit. A quick slash saw a red ribbon across the dog's left flank, enraging him into shredding the guy's arm. Then Barky went for his groin. The man's screams were blood curdling.

Shea was holding his own; he wanted to go the distance with this wanker. The bout ended prematurely when Faith knocked the guy unconscious with the business end of a cane off one of the displays.

"Barky, off!"

"Oh my God, call an ambulance!"

TRIUMPH

Chapter 24
Sunday, 3 June

Flashes of white light
The light goes through what I see
Colored thought waves,
visions of poetry

I t was twenty years ago today. Nope, that's not right, that's a song. It was ten years ago today. Yeah, that's it. At Cooper's Food Hall, in the City Centre. The day five became one. The day they all looked back on as 'The Day.'

Dani, Luke, Ben, and Cy, having lunch, in town less than a month. Luke spotting Abbas, his old friend and school chum. That was the beginning, nothing came before. Ten years.

The first day of the next ten years broke sunny and calm, the second week of a hopefully long, warm summer. The Fab Five were under the yew, tightening the laces on their trainers.

Ten years ago they ran most days together, Cyril in the lead, getting to know their adopted new city. Today's route would take them to the river and back on a circular route, on streets they now knew by heart.

They started north, past Greenbank Primary, where Bashir taught, and accessed Ullet Road by way of Smithdown, heading west then southwest, skirting the north side of Sefton Park. This took them to within view of the Mersey, where they turned to the southeast, generally following its path.

Turning back towards the north, they took Jericho Lane to Elmswood and cut over to Mossley Hill Road, which became Greenbank Road at Penny Lane.

"That felt great!"

"I'm good and loose now."

"Ready for lunch."

"What say you, Dani?"

"I love my boys!"

It was a day of celebration, a day for the gang to thumb their noses at recent events, to dismiss the bad actors of the world and their evil intentions.

The plan was for a light lunch. Get cleaned up, loll about for a bit. Then, around three, pack up the kids and hike up to the Dovey for a Sunday roast and some music. Let the whole tribe follow their muse.

It was quite a procession making its way up Penny Lane a few hours later, led by Miss Rose Ardavan, looking like a dancer on 'Hullabaloo'. Like most Scouse girls, she had a strong sense of style.

Her entourage trailed behind, led by her bodyguards. The youngest, Gabe, Jake, and Caspar, strutted beside their heroes, Cyrus and Shea. Halfway down the lane Ben scooped Gabe up onto his shoulders, the distance a bit much for his short legs.

Faith and Dani walked together, sorting out singing duties for later, Poppy in a papoose. Obs and Robs were discussing the set list.

Luke was getting the skinny on Cyril and Colleen's nuptials; it was like working on a crossword puzzle with no clues. Penny and Bashir amusedly looked on.

Bringing up the rear were Cheryl and Hassan, arm in arm, as was Kevin and Aleah, Neff wondering what this wondrous collective would come up with next.

"Where's Cye?" Gilly asked, welcoming everyone.

"Gone to America," Bashir answered. "He's got a job in Florida, and staying with Ben's folks."

"Thank heavens! I've a new girl on, one I'd like to keep for more than a minute!"

"But Gillian, what about Seamus? He's discovered the fairer sex of late."

"Not an issue. This one would eat the poor boy alive."

It was just Gilly and Emma, the new hire, on today. Faith and Colleen offered to pitch in if needed.

Robin and Abbas went to stow their instruments in the performance hall before eating.

"Hello Geoff!"

"Oy, there's the cultured couple!" he said, sharing a cuddle with Robin.

"Looks like you've got this under control."

"It's me roadie roots! Setting the stage, creating the vibe."

"Looks great!" And it did. P.A. system, three mics, amps, speakers, and the board. Geoff's bass and acoustic guitar were stage right. Three spots, some candles, and a mirror ball. Ben went ballistic if anyone said the word 'disco.' Completing the look and feel were some rugs, tapestries, and a new, very large oil painting of abstract design. Very trippy.

"Wow!"

"Emma did that."

"Emma?"

"Emma Cross, the new waitress. Something else, she is. Come on, we're all set here. Let's eat."

A traditional Sunday roast is a wonderful thing. Beef, potatoes, veggies, gravy, and Yorkshire pudding. Man oh man!

"Alright Colly, out with it. How did you manage to tie the knot so suddenly. And in Portugal, no less!"

"Oh Gilly, it was like a dream. And a complete surprise, after five years! Honestly, I don't think Cyril had any idea himself. Maybe when he saw that little church in Sitio. Anyway, the fourth day there we went up to the fort that overlooks the ocean after dinner. That's where he proposed. Then, three days later, he had it all arranged, church, preacher, and paperwork. Its name was the Sanctuary of Our Lady of Nazaré, a gorgeous place with lots of tile work and a hand painted wooden ceiling. The priest's name was Father Silvino, such a kind old man. And our witnesses were two surfer dudes from Brazil. They did the translating."

"That's so romantic!"

"Well, the rest of the wedding night? Not so romantic. We partied with a bunch of surfers on the beach, most of them recognized Cy. Things got wild, we watched the sun come up, then we surfed before breakfast."

"Brilliant!"

At the next table over Faith was bragging on Barky and Shea. Geoff spellbound over her account of the incident.

"And Barky knew, from the start, there was danger. He snuck up behind those two, quiet as ya like, just waiting for the signal."

"Corr!"

"I think he would've acted if things got violent," Shea said. "That noise he made scared me!"

"Shea didn't hesitate either. As soon as the big bastard let him go to deal with Barky, he clattered hell out of the other one."

"I hear they both ended up in the ozzy."

"Yeah, mum called the ambulance as well as the police. The tall one was concussed, I thought the other one would bleed to death. Ya know that saying the Yanks use, 'tore him a new asshole?' Well, I'll leave it as that."

"Blimey. Good on you though, son!" He clapped Shea on the shoulder. "How about the dog?"

"Again, a lot of blood. Just superficial, thankfully. Luke came by and took him to Dani for some stitches and antibiotics, the filthy wankers!"

"Never a dull moment with this lot."

Over by the taps a certain Miss Emma Cross was wowing the customers, slinging suds and banter. She was a fair lass, late twenties, one to look you straight in the eye. She'd impressively volunteered to go over to the children's table, where she coolly saw them properly sat down with napkins in laps, and using only inside voices. Gilly was giddy.

It was an atmosphere full of warmth and good cheer, a proper English pub. The Greenbank gang comprised nearly half of those present; the rest were mostly from the neighborhood, a family type feel because it was Sunday. There were those on Merseyside in on Dovedale Towers' reputation for music. People were filtering in now in anticipation of some tasty tunes.

Total headcount at showtime was over seventy, all but a dozen or so now situating themselves in the performance hall.

"There he is!" Robin said, embracing Paul. "The band's all here!"

Paul Pilnick, famed Scouser sideman, former member of Stealer's Wheel, and one damned good guitarist. The Eclectibles lineup was ever changing, a true musician's collective. Tonight's ensemble was a sextet. Abbas and Robin were flute and violin, Geoff bass and acoustic six-string guitar, Paul electric and acoustic twelve-string guitar. Faith and Dani were singing leads; both could bang a tambourine, shake a maraca, or smack a cowbell. Geoff and Paul could add vocals. Robin and Abbas, nope.

The house lights were dimmed, Abbas took center stage.

"Hello everyone, welcome to the Dovey. We'd like to begin with something for all the children, a sort of a story in song. Come on kids, come up front and hear the tale of 'Pressed Rat and Warthog.'"

Lucas nearly laughed out loud. Surely the parents in the room were aghast. What kind of nightmares would come after a tale about vermin and beasts?

It was an old Cream song, the title characters the good guys, victimized by a Captain Badman. Geoff told the story in an exaggerated Dickensian lilt:

Pressed Rat and Warthog have closed down their shop
They didn't want to; twas all they had got
Selling atonal apples, amplified heat
And Pressed Rat's collection of doglegs and feet

Musically, the tune's first verse was a simple melody, carried by Abbas and Robin. The second verse added Paul's counter play, bar chords emphasizing the melody, shadowed by Geoff's bass notes. All five verses were alternating combinations of the same progression:

Sadly, they left, telling no one goodbye

Pressed Rat wore red jodhpurs, Warthog a striped tie.
Between them, they carried a three-legged sack
Went straight round the corner, and never came back

The children were mesmerized. Who knew what visions their little brains were calling up:

The bad captain madman had ordered their fate
He laughed and stomped off with a nautical gate
The gate turned into a Deroga tree
And his peg leg got woodworm and broke into three

The bad captain's fate was cheered by all. Hopefully the children would suffer no further worry.

The song paired well with Sweetwater's 'Through an Old Storybook.' This really was a good arrangement, Abbas and Robin only with Faith, Dani, Geoff, and Paul all singing.

The same general pastoral, sort of baroque style, was heightened with the selection of the Grateful Dead's 'Sage and Spirit.' An instrumental, it would fit right in with any chamber music group's repertoire. Both acoustic guitars were utilized, Abbas' flute highlighting the melody.

The mini set ended in similar style, albeit punched up a bit. 'Life is a Long Song,' Ian Anderson's penned words to the wise, stirred the senses. Two verses and choruses, Dani sang the first. Faith the second, the instrumentation just Paul and Geoff, skipping along. Then a slight restart, just before Abbas' flute solo. Pure class. Then Robin adding another layer for the last verse and chorus, both girls singing. Very well received. The band broke, everyone chatted, went to the head, fresh pints, and a doob in the field behind the pub for those who wanted to partake.

Emma was impressed. "I nearly forgot about my customers!" She sought out and introduced herself to Robin. "Excellent! You and the flute player should try out for the Phil!"

Twenty minutes later everyone was back in the hall, anxious for more.

"We've got a surprise for you folks," Abbas announced.

"Is it Paul McCartney?"

"You guys are spoiled! No, Paul and Linda had to pass, but we have got Cyrus and Neff! They've a bit of poetry for you, a point counter point kinda thing. Cy?"

This was a first for the boy, he looked a little sheepish. What the hell, he knew most everyone there.

"My poem is called 'At Odds.'" He cleared his throat:

The world is so confusing, though I try with all my might.
So I put it under my pillow, but it keeps me up at night.
Still, I wonder and worry, what it's all about.
And if I'll sort it out. The End.

Instant applause, and lots of it along with some oohs and aahs.

Cyril nudged Neff. "Tough act to follow."

"Quite." He took the stage.

"My poem is called 'Not to Worry.'"

A child's mind, full of wonder,
The deeds of man, seek to plunder.
Bide your time with innocent pursuits,
Always seeking out the truth.
For wisdom will allay the fright,
Of things that go bump in the night. The End.

The crowd reacted. Some clapped, some cheered, some giggled. Good ole Neff.

The Eclectibles retook the stage and got psychedelic with 'Sacrifice of the Moon (in Four Parts),' originally recorded by Ultimate Spinach. It was an instrumental, the first part up-tempo, flute and violin augmenting the guitar and bass structure. The middle movements slowed the pace, recalling some of the first set's motif. Then the last section, driving to the end.

The next two songs featured vocals. Dani first with the Doors' 'Indian Summer,' backed by the band's dreamy soundscape:

I love you the best, better than all the rest,
That I meet in the summer, Indian summer.

Faith's selection was Gentle Giants' 'Aspirations,' a challenge for most any singer. Instrumentation was straight forward: melodic, but plaintive. Faith supplied the flourish with her voice, sweet and hopeful.

In your hands, holding everyone's future and fate,
It is all in you.

Her pleas were powerful, though softly delivered. You could hear a pin drop:

Be our guide, our light, and our way of life.
And let the world see the way we lead our way.
Hopes, dreams, dreaming that all our sorrows,
Gone forever.

It took a couple of seconds for the audience to react, as if under a spell. Then they loudly showed their appreciation.

The show ended with Traffic's 'Hidden Treasure,' keeping with the evening's general theme. Dani did the honors:

Message in the deep, from a strange eternal sleep,
That is waiting there, that is waiting there,
For you, like hidden treasure.

Plus, it ended with a long, kick-ass instrumental!

CHAPTER 25
THURSDAY, 7 JUNE

I have finally found a way to live
In the colour of the Lord

Missives from Merseyside
Liverpool Anglican Cathedral

Hello, my name is Dorothy Spittle, from Friary Cottage, in *Denbigh. It's not far from Liverpool, just the other side of the river Dee, in North Wales. It's a lovely little town, with a fine castle. We call it Dinbych, which means 'Little Fortress.' The Clwydia Hills are nearby, very pretty, they are.*

My craft is ecclesiastical embroidery, and I made frontals for the Anglican Cathedral for eighteen years. My time there began in '54, and I'm retired now, just me and my two little dogs, my dearies.

I suppose not everyone knows what a frontal is. Actually, they do, everyone that's ever been in a church of any kind. A frontal is an altar cloth, the drapery, I guess you could say, that adorns the front of the altar. They help set the mood for the service, designed to invoke the feel of the occasion. Consistency is important, despite the variety of colors and sizes. There are guidelines, certain symbols and images at the proper time of year. Quite intricate they can be, I spent two years on one frontal alone.

I consider myself very lucky, a useful career, serving God in my own way, creating something to last. I still come back from time to time, to visit my students who carry on the work. Such a wonderful place.

Ben had been taken with Dorothy Spittle, a kind, pious soul so grateful for her rather uncomplicated lot in life. He'd conducted two interview sessions and found her to be very attentive and forthcoming. She'd sit there, on a bench in the Cathedral Gardens, bright eyes behind those big, black framed glasses, her two shih-tzus sniffing about, telling her story. Her work was beautiful. He'd considered using one of her pieces for the book, but in the end, decided to shoot the entire scene.

Right now, Ben was on the roof of a different church, St. Brides. Five quid to a maintenance worker was the price for access.

What a view! Three blocks due east of the cathedral, it sat at the corner of Percy and Huskisson. It was nine in the morning on a clear day, the sun illuminating fully the cathedral and its grounds, perched atop St. James Mount.

The lens he'd chosen afforded a view of the entire complex. He'd picked the east side of the property for aesthetics; there were no buildings in the foreground, just the gardens and structure itself.

The sun was still low enough to enhance the reddish hue of the cathedral, made of sandstone mined at nearby Woolton. It almost glowed. The nave was at the north end, to his right. The tower was central, with transepts on each side. The Chapel House occupied the south end, next to the Choir Chamber and Great Porch. Massive!

It occurred to Ben to include a chapter of his own in the book, a sort of essay, describing his experiences creating the book. He could include the odd fact and tidbit picked up along the way. For example, the cathedral's chief architect, Giles Gilbert Scott, was knighted for his efforts. He also designed the iconic red telephone box!

CHAPTER 26
SUNDAY, 24 JUNE

Merging with a grain of sand
Try hard to catch us if you can

They were tired, sore, sandy, wind-blown, and a little sunburned. It was great! They were also hungry and thirsty. A day on the water will do that to you.

Astrid, Cye, and Ian were spending the weekend together in St. Pete. There was plenty of room at the Pines house on Lake Pasadena, Gene and Louise were in Liverpool. Astrid drove up from Sarasota Friday afternoon. All three of them had the weekend off.

Deciding on the Chattaway for a refueling spot, they loaded up the canoe and gear in Gene's old pickup and headed crosstown.

It had been a long paddle, circumnavigating the entirety of Mullet Key, which was almost all of Fort Desoto State Park, occupying the south end of Pinellas County. Ian was still getting used to all that was central Florida's gulf coast; Cye simply thought himself to be on another planet. Astrid was right at home, her chosen milieu.

The Chattaway was an old school Florida family bar and grill with indoor and outdoor accommodations and lots of kitschy yard art. And good food!

Sam, short for Samantha, greeted them with a smile. They went there a lot.

"So, a Venezuelan, an Iranian, and an Englishman walk into a bar." They all had a giggle.

The fare was the usual, almost. Water and beer were substituted for milkshakes to pair with fries and Chattacheeseburgers. It hit the spot. All that was lacking now was a shower.

Ian had cooked on Friday evening, grilled snapper with rice and asparagus, and the three just sat around with a couple of bottles of wine and caught up. Ian was pretty much in a routine now, school, the symphony, and American life. Just because you speak the same language, basically, does not mean assimilation into a new culture would be smooth. Now he knew better the challenges Lucas and the gang in Liverpool had faced.

Cye was settling in quite nicely. He was more accustomed to the Americans and their ways, his acclimation easier due to his exposure back home in Tehran. He'd gotten two offers from his three job interviews, opting for a position with Davis Designs. It was an established firm, its roots tracing back to 1912 in Lincoln, Nebraska, where it still maintained an office, as well as Vermillion, South Dakota. St. Pete was its newest branch, located in the Kenwood district, between downtown and the western suburbs. Davis had a stellar reputation. Cye was excited.

He'd bought a car, a used Camaro convertible. It was 'way cool!' When in Rome, right? The Pines wouldn't allow him to pay rent. Ian said don't even try. But they were figuring out how to help their hosts in other ways. Such kind people, Cye would never forget how Gene helped Luke get his folks out of Iran.

Astrid was in her groove. She was twenty-five years old, had her own place, a dream job, and would be awarded a master's degree before Christmas. She had always been a good student, it came easy to her, and she always hungered for more. She also possessed a strong intellect, and she knew climbing the ladder to success did not guarantee happiness. Weekends like this were necessary, a chance to unwind and be with friends. She felt as long as she had her priorities in place, and kept business before pleasure, she could cut loose from time to time, even fuck up now and then.

She liked Ian. No, she loved Ian, they'd become very close. For a while she thought what it might be like to take him as a lover. There was an age difference, he was to turn twenty in the fall, but that didn't matter. He was more mature than most all the boys her own age she'd gone to school with. She valued his friendship and didn't want to complicate things.

Cye, of course, was different. Older than her, and a completely different background. Exotically handsome, though, and whip smart. An academic, like her. Their friendship seemed solid already, time would tell. He seemed focused on his new life here, thankful for the opportunity. It was hard to imagine all he'd been through.

Last night the three of them went to Tampa Stadium, the 'Big Sombrero,' to watch the Tampa Bay Rowdies host the San Jose Earthquakes. The North American Soccer League wasn't on the level with the English first division, or any of the big European leagues, but it was pretty damn entertaining. The Tampa club had cheerleaders, scantily dressed buxom beauties, along with Krazy George. They also had a fan club, Ralph's Mob, and a theme song declaring soccer to be a kick in the grass.

Ian didn't like the schedule; the league played its games in the summer, the opposite of the rest of the world. The squads were weird as well, mostly young Americans that included players from Mexico and the Caribbean, and some bonified world stars, albeit in the twilight of their careers. Still, it was a treat to see icons such as Pele, Cruyff, and Beckenbauer in person.

There was a scattering of British players also, Terry Darracott from Everton playing for Tulsa, and Roger Kenyon, Cyril's mate, was now in Vancouver. The Rowdies had, amongst others, Rodney Marsh, the 'Clown Prince' of soccer. Last night's match was a good one, the home team prevailing three-two.

The spent trio made their way back home. Astrid took an armload inside and went to bathe, while the guys unloaded and washed off the canoe.

"She fancies you, mate," Ian said, continuing he and Cye's conversation.

"Really, are you sure?"

"No, she is a female, that would be impossible. But I'm seeing interest from both sides. Am I right?"

"She's really something."

"She's got it all, maybe even smarter than you, if that's possible. And much better looking!"

Cye smiled. "What should I do?"

"Be bolder than your brother, Abbas. Robin pretty much had to spell it out for him. Talk to her before she goes home, tell her you want to come down to Sarasota, get to know her world."

Now Cye laughed. "And you're not even twenty yet. You've been around Lucas too long!"

CHAPTER 27
MONDAY, 25 JUNE

Secret agent man
Secret agent man
They've given you a number,
and taken away your name

It was half past seven on a gorgeous evening on Merseyside, the sun's influence waning as dusk was making its claim on the day. Hassan, Ben, and Luke were hearing what Eugene Pine was saying, but were too stunned to speak. Finally, Lucas managed to blurt out one simple question.

"They want me to what?"

"Join the Company."

"The Company. You mean the CIA?"

"We don't use that term, generally."

"We?" Ben asked.

"That's why you're here, Ben. It's time to come clean. I was a field agent before transferring over to the diplomatic corps. That changed after you were born. Lou and I decided to keep our family together.

Besides, it was time, it's a job you break from before you stack up too many enemies, on either side."

They were in the garden, middle house in the row. Just to the south, on the other side of the stone wall at Neff's, Louise was holding court, Aleah, Faith, and Dani her subjects. Much had been discussed.

Faith's pregnancy, she was now showing. No, no names yet, was the first item to be reported on. Poppy Anne was next; such a little angel was the verdict. Then she grilled Aleah. How was Hassan, how was she, how were they adjusting to their new life in England.

She then gave updates from her side of the pond.

"Cye hit the ground running. Personally, I think he was suddenly afforded an opportunity, although because of horrible circumstances, and realized he was more than capable of making a life for himself in a new land. I really can draw comparisons to Astrid, who has seized the day herself. They're both so intelligent!"

Then she laughed, "I just hope they both decide to smell the roses along the way. They're both so driven. Out in the 'real world' I think they're still both quite young."

"Ian's quite different," she continued, "he's a smart kid, don't be fooled. He works hard and is very responsible. But his eyes are always open, he seems very savvy. I love his personality; I think spending his adolescence around the folks here was invaluable. They all send their love, by the way."

And so on and so forth. When the subject changed to those last days in Tehran, however, Louise became somewhat reticent, claiming not to always being in the loop on what Gene was doing and the particulars of Luke's movements.

"It's okay Louise," Dani said, "Lucas told me everything, finally. Everyone knows but the younger children."

"Oh, good for him. You shouldn't have secrets in a marriage, they tend to fester. It was amazing, what he did and how he went about it. Let me tell you, some very important people took notice."

On the other side of the wall Eugene continued to explain, "Luke, your interview at the embassy, it made some people sit up, take notice."

"Which interview, I had four."

"Really?"

"Yeah, once inside the gate, then two in the holding area, no names given. Then with Colonel Holland in the cafeteria."

"Okay, the second one inside. That guy, he was with the Company."

"I'm not surprised, he and I danced for a while."

"Well, he'd gone to the sergeant at the gate and got a full report. He'd already heard your little chat with the liaison. Live, by the way, he was listening in and looking on."

"I figured it was a two-way mirror."

"And, before they could meet with the regular embassy personnel and decide what to do, Ben and I had hit them with the one-two punch of General Jablonski and the school higher-ups."

He continued, "You've been on their minds ever since. I was 'requested' to come here, Lucas. We flew from Tampa to D.C. and were escorted to Langley. The new station chief in Tehran is Tom Ahern, he's there now. I spoke with William Daugherty. He's to be the new Operations Director in Iran. He made the pitch. Almost everything you did during those five days was straight out of the handbook, Luke. After they figured out you weren't one of theirs, or anyone else's, they were salivating. You're the right age, speak the language, know the city, and are resourceful and quick on your feet. And stupid brave!"

Lucas paused for a second, it was a lot to take in.

"It's amazing to me how smart these people must be, yet so naïve. Or they don't do their homework. Where would they want me stationed?"

"Tehran, between certain safe houses and the Embassy itself."

"I have a family. Surely they know that."

"They do. You're a potential big prize Luke. They like to cast a wide net. Your language skills are very valuable, they're looking past Iran. South America is always fertile Company ground. In Venezuela, another place close to your heart, Luis Herrera Campins was just, how can I say it, installed as the new president. That guy is a strongman, a wolf in sheep's clothing."

"Damn, I wonder if Dani is aware." He hesitated, "I'm flattered Gene, but no. No way."

"I already told them that. I would have bitched them out, but I tend to agree, you'd be quite the catch. But I know you Luke, and how committed you are to all these wonderful people. And I love Daniela. You're not going anywhere."

"Thanks, Gene. Listen guys, I'll tell Dani about this but otherwise let's hush it, especially with Cyril. He gets wind of this, and I'll never hear the end of it."

CHAPTER 28
FRIDAY, 6 JULY

Considering her past, April Walker was one hell of a bright light. A conversation about her past was a short one, for there was no one that knew a single thing about her that she wasn't aware of. Except for her parents, of course, who dropped her off, as an infant, at a Merseyside police station in the dead of night. That was over twenty-five years ago.

The orphanage taking her in gave her the name April. She had arrived that month, Walker was added when she was adopted by a couple in Blackpool when she was eight years old. It was not a loving, nurturing household; she'd basically grown up on the streets.

Luckily, there was strength, and character, and a fairly true moral compass inside the girl. Now, as a woman, her head was up, her gait proud, she could look anyone straight in the eye.

She'd not had much when she came down to Liverpool, staying in a hostel until catching a big break in meeting Gillian Parry. Gilly took her on at the Dovey and let her stay in the upstairs flat there, the same flat Freddie Mercury stayed in nearly ten years prior.

She still took the odd shift at the pub but was getting fulltime work at Erins Pharmacy, settling in there nicely now after learning the ropes.

Working for the Mason brothers was her best job ever. They were wonderful chaps, learners themselves, leaning on Faith and Colleen's experience, as well as Roisin's business sense and accounting skills. She could see a successful future building for the store. She was determined to do her part.

The best part about her life now was her friends. She'd gotten to know the regulars at the Dovey, folks from the neighborhood. Also the local merchants, workers, and assorted people you see on the street regularly.

She'd fallen in with the Greenbank lot as well. Such nice people, so welcoming and kind. She was at the pharmacy now, counting her cash drawer at the end of the day. Tears came to her eyes; she'd suddenly realized she'd not only carved out a life for herself, people actually cared about her.

"April, luv, you okay?"

She smiled, "Never better, Faith. Tears of joy!"

"Fabulous! Come on then, it's been a long week, let's get naughty!"

"I heard that!" said Colleen, coming out from the back, "Count me in. Come on, boys, it's the weekend!"

Barky and Seamus led the way back down Penny Lane.

The scene on Greenbank revealed a row house divided. Bashir and Penny, along with Rosie and Caspar, Neff, Aleah, and Hassan, had gone over by Sefton Park to the Stillwell's for dinner. George and Rose had some item of interest to discuss with Neff and Hassan. Very hush-hush.

Everyone else was present and accounted for and divided into two groups. Cyrus and the men were in the park, playing football, Otter included. Seamus and Barky joined the fray.

The ladies joined Dani and Cheryl at Robin and Faith's. Pleasantries exchanged, they immediately went up to the attic for a buzz. Faith abstained, staying downstairs to watch the children.

"Just one for me, girls. I tend to get a bit stupid," Cheryl said.

The plan was for a potluck cookout in the garden out back, courtesy of the ladies, the boys' only duty grilling the burgers and dogs. It was also decided to do it up American style, only two days after the fourth. No doubt jokes about the war for independence would ensue.

Colleen was in charge of recipes for the side dishes, potato salad, carrot and raisin salad, and in particular, baked beans.

"You people just open a can of Heinz and plop it down, sometimes cold. Ya gotta give it some backbone. Mustard, brown sugar or molasses, and some pork, for goodness' sake!"

Robin had iced down a couple of cases of lager. The girls helped themselves and prepared the sides while Jake, Gabe, and Isaac played in the front room, Poppy looking on from the bassinet.

Isaac was a smart little terrier, now six years old, and had settled himself down, no longer the manic, yappy, jack-in-the-box. He was very much duty bound, however, sounding off at the first sign of something untoward.

Faith had made herself a cup of herbal tea. The baby was on her mind a lot of late. All she had to do was look down and be reminded of the passing time. She went over and looked out the front window at the scene across the street.

"Boys never fully grow up, do they?"

"They never fully mature, that's for certain," Cheryl agreed.

"Their brain stops growing before their bodies," April pointed out.

"At least something worthwhile gets bigger," said Robin with a grin. "Dani, how did you manage it back at the start, just you and those four hooligans?"

"It was an adventure, especially staying in that hotel room for, I don't know, seemingly forever. Penny and Bashir came to the rescue, and Penny sorted the boys right out. The Governess, she was."

"And it took the lot of you to sort my boys out!" Cheryl chimed. "Or, at least point them in the right direction."

"I think your passions, each of you, inspired them but I'd wager they were always good, well-behaved kids," Colleen remarked.

"Spot on!" agreed Robin.

"And now Ian, Shea, and Cy can return the favor," Dani said. "Soon there'll be six young'uns ten and under scurrying about. The neighbors will think we're running a day care center!"

"April, are you sure you want to get mixed up in this menagerie?" Faith asked.

"Well, it is entertaining, if a bit confusing, at times. But no, I'm happy to be around your families. It's different than I'm used to, for sure. You girls have been so kind, I'll take it, warts and all. I'm just sorry Cye packed himself off to America. He's so dreamy!"

"Amen!" Cheryl sighed. "And, after Faith and Colly, you'd be the third bird to be snatched from the Dovey's nest."

"Hey, what's all the laughter about?"

"Baba!" shouted Gabe. Abbas and Ben were home. Robin was on it.

"Okay you two, I see ya. Now go and get cleaned up before I smell ya. And what are you grinning about?"

"Abbas nutmegged Cyril!"

"Brilliant, now we can all sleep well. Go on then!" They both skipped upstairs.

"Well done!" said April.

"Yeah, well, now the real babysitting begins, all hands to the pump!"

CHAPTER 29
THURSDAY, 12 JULY

Yesterday in crannies or in nooks you will not find
Yesterday in chronicles or books you will not find
All you see of yesterday is shadows in your mind

Ben longed for the old days. It seemed odd, such melancholy from a man not yet thirty years of age. Maybe it was just the knowledge that the world changed at its own pace, rewarding those bringing about the new, and ignoring those still coming to terms with the old. How to find balance was the challenge.

That struggle, mirrored in everyday life in a myriad of ways, was to be the approach to his latest assignment, a retrospective on pop culture in the seventies.

His first thought was a simple three-word article, 'Disco still Sucks!' Perhaps John, his editor, would ask for a little more detail.

Music was a good place to start. All of the creative arts were fertile ground for new ideas, new ways to express oneself. Ben considered the latter half of the sixties as his golden age. The British invasion's trippy side heralded a boom of psychedelia in various genres, blurring the lines between pop, rock, blues, and jazz. LPs replaced 45s on college radio in the states and pirate radio wherever it existed.

Folk music had a revival with the newly coined singer-songwriter, and old school country sharpened its spurs, going alternate and outlaw.

Now, on the brink of the eighties, the purer forms still and would always remain, such as classical, jazz, and the blues. Rock was still being reinvented, and the seventies had seen the rise of new wave and disco.

Disco wasn't going away anytime soon. Bands like Abba, Donna Summer, the Bee Gees, and Kool and the Gang were topping the charts. The phenomena had given rise to an entire lifestyle, played out in films like *Saturday Night Fever*, and celebrated at Club 54.

Punk and new wave were also not exactly Ben's cup of tea, but at least he understood the passion behind the movement. A bit extreme, he felt. Some of those kids looked like they had dived headfirst into someone's tackle box.

The term 'classic rock' had arisen. Giving something such a defining term meant that an era had been established, and was coming to a close. It was true. Bands like Pink Floyd, the Eagles, and Led Zeppelin appeared to be on the fade.

Technology fueled change, in every possible way. Recording on tape was the in-studio industry standard for music. The public got to first hear the music on tape with reel-to-reel players, followed by eight-tracks and cassettes. The newest innovation was the Sony Walkman, a personal cassette player with earphones.

Technology was making its mark in the cinema as well, giving film makers lots of new creative toys. This was graphically proven to Ben last month when he saw a too real looking alien creature bust out of Harry Dean Stanton's chest.

Changes in literature during the '70s were a little more behind the scenes. Writers saw their work published more efficiently and distributed more easily as a result of advanced printing capabilities. Readers did find a new way to enjoy their favorite author's work, the audio book, with someone to read the material to them.

Finally, no narrative on pop culture would be complete without a discussion on fashion. The way people present themselves to the world is one of the most constant yet confusing enigmas contained within the human condition.

Scholars will tell you that the earliest humans were motivated by the desire to survive with respect to their appearance. They wanted to stay warm, hide from predators, and hunt for food. Philosophers will tell you things haven't changed at all; it's just a lot more complicated now. We still want to stay warm, but we need to be color coordinated when we do so. We fear predators, so we look tough, and unconcerned. We need to eat, so we look hungry, the kind of hunger that attracts those that can feed us.

And so, we trade wool for down, get tattoos, take on a menacing air, and dress for success. It was a question of survival.

Ben looked back over his notes, satisfied that he'd covered the main points of his account. A fair amount of space would be required to cover sports, celebrity, and the common vernacular. A representation of the decade's fads would be a nice touch; you wouldn't want to forget important icons such as slinkies, Nehru jackets, shags, and the Freddy.

One thing for sure, the last line of his article would be his first thought on the subject. Disco still sucks!

CHAPTER 30
WEDNESDAY, 18 JULY

There's no time to be lost
You'll pay the cost, so get it right

There was no promise made
The part you've played, the chance you took

Rites of passage, no matter the origin or particulars of fulfillment, can occur when least expected. While it's true that most milestone moments are planned for in advance and marked by practiced pomp and ceremony, you never know when the fangs of fate will reach up and bite you in the ass.

One such rite is when a boy becomes a man. This is never achieved in one fell swoop, with a feat accomplished and a certificate bestowed. It happens over time, in fits and starts, with no set schedule.

Seamus hopped in Cyril's Hillman and they headed north, skirting the City Centre on their way to West Derby.

Everton Football Club's Bellefield training ground was humming with activity despite the early hour. It was also humming with anticipation; the day marked one month exactly before the start of the new season. The same scene would unfold on countless pitches across England, all the participants determined to post a good campaign.

The pair entered the main building and split up, Cyril to the Senior Team's changing room, and Seamus over on the other side with the Juniors.

Shea never quite made it through the door; however, the fitness coach met him in the hall. He did not look happy.

"Can I have a word?"

"Good morning. Of course, what is it?"

"I'm sorry Shea, you're not to train this morning. The gaffer wants to see you, right away."

His heart sank. "All right," he mumbled. Still, he found it hard to move.

"Go on then. He's in his office."

He looked into the man's eyes, searching for hope. They were empty. The walk to the manager's office was torturous, two minutes spent in a downward spiral. He was determined, however, to keep his composure.

Gordon Lee sat him down across the desk, his countenance serious. He didn't waste words.

"Seamus, your time here has been well spent. You've kept your head down, trained hard, and got on with your mates. With that said I'm afraid a change will have to be made." He hesitated, apparently troubled as to how to continue. "Tell you what. Come take a walk with me. I need to show you something."

Shea followed glumly down the hall, death march part two. Head down, he wasn't even sure where he was.

Suddenly, somehow, they were in the senior team's room. The atmosphere was typical, blokes getting ready for training, the mood bright, the lads giving each other the mickey. It got quiet then, the team standing together, looking at Gordon and the kid, almost like they were being interrupted.

Then, as if on cue, they separated, right down the middle, leaving a gap that led to a bank of individual stalls, one per player. And there it hung, the eleven shirt, McTimons the name above the number.

Broad smiles broke out on everyone's face but Shea's.

"You bastards!" This was followed by tears, and a grin of his own as Gordon tousled his hair and nudged him towards the scrum.

He trained with a fervor that session, his skipper Mick Lyons cautioning him on reaching for too much.

"Pace yourself, lad. You've made the team; it's a long slog, the next nine months."

His mates on the junior squad hung around and feted Shea afterwards. It was a good sign that the gaffer liked promoting from within. These boys saw in Shea renewed hope for their futures as a result.

Greenbank was over the moon at the news, prompting a bit of embarrassment in the quiet, unassuming middle sibling. His father was beside himself.

"Turn the oven off Cheryl, I'll grab a takeaway on the way back."

"Back from where?"

"The pub. Me and Seamus are going for a pint. What say, lads, my treat?"

Down at the Baltic Fleet, James Doohan slammed his bar towel against the taps.

"Damn it Cyril, look what you've done now!"

CHAPTER 31
WEDNESDAY, 25 JULY

I will pay
day by day
anyway
Lock, bolt, and key

A day in the communal life.

Otter was back from his morning walk, one of his favorite times of the day. The fresh morning smells, dew on the grass, he and brother Barky reestablishing the territory.

Breakfast was also big on the favorites list, hanging out with Luke and Dani and their pups, watching them come to life each morning. Those little whelps sure grew up fast! The male, Jake, was already bossing him around. He didn't mind. Both Jake and Poppy, who was only recently weaned, were his first responsibility.

He used to have a job during the day with Dani, at the place where they helped sick and injured animals. Now it was more important to stay at home. The pack had a lot of young ones now, and he was responsible for their safety. He had a lieutenant, Isaac, his chief scout and source of information. That little dude was hard to train, really antsy, and prone to sound the alarm at the first sniff of something strange. He'd settled well though, and now only came to him with real concerns.

Barky had recently got himself a day job, watching over the business where Faith and Colly worked. This was important. A lot of strangers came there, some needed to be tracked. Also, various members of the pack went there from time to time. Barky had to stay vigilant. And did the pack realize, apart from Faith, that she was going to bear pups in the fall?

He went out front with Luke, got an ear scratch, and lay on the stoop. He liked the sun lighting up the big tree in the park, the birds starting to sing. He would remain there, watching the pack emerge from their dens and go off for the day. Someone would come and fetch him, and he would clock in for his shift.

"Okay Otter, I'm off." Dani had a full day at the clinic planned, the regular patient load and some paperwork to finish. She joined the kiddie caravan Bashir was leading up to Greenbank Primary, six blocks north, beyond which was her bus stop at Smithdown Road. She needed to get in and on it. Millie, the Carver's black lab, was getting spayed this morning.

School hadn't begun yet, by a long shot, but Bashir was the school's Head Teacher, a year-round job in some respects. Rose, Caspar, and Cyrus were in tow, looking to avail themselves of the art supplies and playground. In the upcoming school year only Rose and Caspar would be attending. Cy had just graduated, and Jacob was still a year away.

Cyrus was excited at the thought of attending secondary school, where the range of subjects was immense, compared to the highly structured curriculum he'd experienced so far. His first year there would be his brother Seamus' last. Literature was Cy's magic garden, the place he could dream and plan his own vision of the world. Luke would provide the instruction, Ben the inspiration.

Ben was getting his own dose of inspiration, in the form of one Stephen Shakeshaft, Echo photog extraordinaire. Originally from the Wirral, Stephen started as a copy boy in '62. His rise at the paper ran parallel to his education in the photographic arts, but was not limited to those skills, but rather attributed to his ability to gain access to his subjects and his disarming charm in opening them up.

Now only thirty-three years old, Stephen's body of work was impressive, and immensely varied. A shot of a waif-like street urchin, age five, outside a council high-rise. Cilla Black, sharing a cuddle with her husband, newly married. Sister Marina in the bowels of Walton Prison, smiling, giving succor to those wretched souls. Even Kenny Dalglish, in bed with the latest addition to Liverpool's trophy case, the '77 European Cup.

"We'll need to team up for this gig," Stephen said, sitting across Ben's desk. "Labor strikes are touchy affairs; emotions tend to run high. Our press badges will help at times, sometimes we'll have to stow them."

"You take the lead, I'll take my cues accordingly and watch our backs," Ben offered.

"You stand out in a crowd. I'm not sure, I suppose that can be a boon or a bust."

"The story of my life."

Meanwhile, back at the ranch. Actually, they were defunct riding stables just off Harthill Road near Calderstones Park. Hassan was taking his cues from Neff and George Stillwell, presently talking with the new owner of the property.

This was Hassan's first day back at work, so to speak, and he was thrilled at the prospect of once again being productive. George had come up with the idea; the man knew how to make money, even in hard times.

Wealthy people, particularly those with egos to match their wallets, tended to separate themselves from their peers with ostentatious displays of their financial well-being. Depending on individual tastes and tendencies, this might be achieved with expensive cars, or boats, or exotic young ladies at their side. Or, maybe, a fine manor in which to live. Something to really catch the eye and capture the imagination.

Hassan's architectural sensibilities had run amok since coming to England. He loved driving out and away from the city, to see the different types of buildings, some dating back to medieval times. These structures were being repurposed all the time. It was a good thing, preserving the past. If someone wanted a house made from an old pub, or church, or grist mill, or even stables, why not? He was just the one to design it for them.

And so Ardavan Concepts and Design was born. Hopefully, this first project would get them off the ground, word of mouth would sustain it. George would drum up the clientele and Neff would handle the legalities. It was time to get a dedicated phone line, and order up some business cards.

Speaking of houses, April couldn't walk to work anymore. She was moving, out of the pub and into Ray and Roisin's house, up in Kensington. It was still a good location, just northeast of the University Hospital.

Ray and Clive helped Luke bring her stuff up in the Vauxhall, then left her and Roisin to arrange it.

"It's a wonderful place, Ro! I'm still a bit mousey about it all, though. Are you sure?"

"Nonsense! It's more than big enough, and I'm looking forward to us getting some of the rampant masculinity off the place."

"It is a bachelor's pad, like a pub with an Everton theme."

"Cyril's shirt can stay. The rest, luv, don't worry, we'll sort it."

Co-conspirators, united by circumstance, allied in a common cause. It looked like the beginning of a long, close friendship.

A few miles away, a different segment of the Greenbank gang was allied for a common cause. The occasion called for business attire and a proper grooming. The participants now seated in the outer office of the honorable Mister Philip Carter, now chairman of the board at Everton Football Club.

Born in Glasgow, young Philip came to Liverpool with his father after his mother's death, and was educated in the city before serving in the RAF in the mid '40s.

Carter's big break came after the war. He caught the eye of John Moores while working at Littlewoods Department Stores, and became his protégé, rising through the ranks to managing director. Moores also invited him onto Everton's board. Last year, after Moores' retirement, Carter took over as chairman.

Seamus McTimons was a mix of emotions. This was the day he dreamed of, yet he felt strangely uncomfortable. He would walk out of this place a professional footballer, he just needed to calm down, embrace the process. A part of growing up, just like his mum and dad said.

The chairman asked his secretary to show the McTimons in and stepped around his desk to greet them.

Shea showed his mother through the door, followed by his father and both Lucas and Jacob Carter. You could have knocked the venerable Philip Carter over with a feather.

"Hi cuz!" What an icebreaker.

Luke and Philip knew each other, meeting first at Cyril's contract negotiations, then from time to time at matches or team functions. They had a mutual respect for the club and its people, and therefore had developed a genuine friendship, despite their supposed adversarial roles at times like these.

"Ah, Lucas Carter, hello, sir. And just how, may I ask, do you know young master McTimons?"

"He's my next-door neighbor."

"Just my luck."

Luke ceded the floor to Shea.

"These are my parents, Mister Chairman, Kevin and Cheryl McTimons. Mum, Dad, Mister Philip Carter." It was the most words the boy had spoken in weeks.

"I'm pleased to meet you both. We're very fond of Shea here at the club. We don't make this commitment easily. It's not just good footballers we want, quality of character is a must. Your son is a fine young man."

"Thank you, sir," Kevin replied. "His mother's kept him on the straight and narrow. He's always wanted to be a footballer, but he's young. I want him looked after, mind you."

The chairman took notice.

Luke chimed in, "We have a thought or two along those lines," he began.

"I can imagine. But first things first. Who's this strapping young lad?"

"Oh, I'm sorry, Philip, this is my son, Jacob. Jake?"

"Pleased to meet you, sir," offering his hand.

"Hello, Jacob. And are you an Everton supporter, as well?"

"Up the Blues!"

"Lucas, they tell me Cyril was recently married. Are your families still living together?"

"Yes, it's quite cozy. I believe you know that our friends and families have occupied an entire rowhouse down in Mossley Hill?"

"Indeed. It seems quite the collection of characters."

"Yeah, well, we're all having babies now. I'm thinking of starting my own little football academy. We could produce the next generation of Toffees."

"Hopefully I'll be retired by then! All right then, back to business. You have concerns?"

"Not really," Luke replied. "I know the club has a pretty set wage structure in regard to junior players coming up. We'd like to see Shea at the top end of that scale, given his ability and potential. What we'd really like is a promise not to loan him out to another club, until he's at least eighteen. This will give him a chance to finish school, I'm one of his teachers, by the way, and to mature more fully. The lad's still growing."

"Seems reasonable. He's obviously in a good environment, better to leave it be. Of course, the manager and his staff will determine how much playing time Shea gets. He could sit a lot, you should know."

"Shea?" Kevin asked.

"Not a problem sir. I'll earn my way."

"Well said. Okay, let's put pen to paper. I'll have Cate bring us some tea."

An hour later they were on the street, headed for the car park. The 'Fixer' had done his job well. Shea had inked the most lucrative contract ever given to a junior call up.

"He earned it all by himself," Luke told Kevin and Cheryl. "I just greased the wheels."

Cheryl reached up and kissed him, followed by a fierce hug.

"You drew blood from the turnip," she declared. "Come on boys, let's go down to the Baltic Fleet for a pint. I'm buying."

"No mum," Shea said. "This one's on me."

CHAPTER 32
WEDNESDAY, 1 AUGUST

Nothing is real
And nothing to get hungabout
Strawberry Fields forever

Ben had a lot of photos of the iconic gates at the entrance to Strawberry Field. His favorite was taken back in '69, on his first visit there. It featured Dani and Luke, standing together in front of the gothic red structure, anchored on each side by stone pillars, rich with graffiti. It was early days, before the couple realized they were a couple.

It wasn't the right choice for the book, though. He needed something simpler. Just the gates themselves, framed by the surrounding vegetation. Lighting was key to the image, and the location was challenging in this respect. Then it hit him. He needed a photograph with the light coming from behind the gates, normally the opposite of how you would approach a subject.

The reason for this had to do with the fact that most of the trees on this immense property were near the stone walls that surrounded it.

Near the gates themselves the trees overhung the space, making for poor lighting at the entrance.

The gates lay in basically an east-west running section of wall, which meant the sun would follow that line each day. That meant that the winter solstice, the twenty-first of December, would find old Sol on its most southern arc.

His prints and negatives were filed by subject and date, thankfully, and in short order he'd found the one. In retrospect, he was surprised he hadn't appreciated the photo more.

It was shot in mid-November '72, in the early afternoon. He remembered the occasion, an unusually warm but windy day. He had stood by the curb on Beaconsfield, left of center to the gates, no one around. Fallen leaves made for a carpet on the pavement, tree branches framing the gates.

It was the light that made the image, transforming the scene into something from a fable. There was no direct light, the trees filtering the sun's energy into an illuminating glow, creating an aura within the space. Intermittent beams of light found their way through the canopy, and the ones that shone through the gates themselves were ethereal, like little messages from heaven.

Deciding on an angle for the chapter's text had been a struggle. The place had a history. Two wealthy merchants had owned the estate before it was sold in the '30s to the Salvation Army for a children's home, only to be demolished in '73 due to its poor condition. All that was fairly common knowledge, what Ben wanted was a more personal account.

Enter the 'Fixer.' Luke taught at Quarry Bank Comprehensive School, where John Lennon, the reason Strawberry Field was so well known, studied as a teen in the '50s. Luke knew Dave Bennion, who was a pupil there then and now taught there. Dave turned him on to Margie Bracewell, both a schoolmate and neighbor of Lennon's.

Ben's interview with Margie was gold; she was charming, witty, and forthcoming with her past connection to the former Beatle.

Setting aside the print, he picked up the text to proofread it one last time.

Missives from Merseyside
Strawberry Field

Hey all! I'm Margaret Bracewell, but Margie's my name. I'm from Woolton, so Strawberry Field has always been a part of my life, we lived very close by on Kenilworth.

The old place always scared me when I was just a little girl, my mum saying if I didn't mind meself I'd end up in the children's home. Then the Salvation Army, which owned the estate, would throw a garden party in the summer and invite the neighborhood. Such a big place, with a fine old mansion!

Of course, it's famous now. John Lennon wrote a song about it, very personal to him, it was. I knew his Aunt Mimi long before I met him, she and mum took tea together quite often. Mimi lived on Menlove, just around the corner from us.

I met John when he came to live with his aunt, and we both went to Quarry Bank school. He was a year older and always in trouble, it seemed. Fighting, smoking, and cursing were his subjects; it's a wonder he wasn't expelled. I suppose the headmaster, Mr. Pobjoy, was the reason. He encouraged John's interest in music, resulting in him going to the Liverpool College of Art.

At Quarry Bank he told me about how he would sneak into Strawberry Field and play with the kids there. What else went on I don't know but he was repeatedly told to stay out, even taken home to his aunt one day and threatened with hanging if caught again. That's where he came up with the line 'nothing to get hung about.'

John was cheeky, threats didn't faze him one bit; he took me there several times. He fancied me for a while, or maybe just wanted to see how far I'd go with him. Not very far, I can assure you, but, yeah, some affection was shared. I'll leave it at that.

I still live in the area, and go there sometimes. The house was torn down, you can't enter the grounds, but the gates are there. That entrance, that's what you think of. People come there a lot. Oh, such memories!

· · ·

Ben set the piece aside. What a gem this lady was, and a journalist's dream! Untold stories of the Beatles were increasingly rare, and this was quite a coup. A writer with a more relaxed set of ethics would take advantage of a person like Margie, but he'd been charmed by this woman still living close by, unmarried, working as a clerk in a solicitor's office on Smithdown, near Erins Pharmacy. He'd taken enough from her; she had shared her story on her terms and that was the end of it.

CHAPTER 33
SATURDAY, 4 AUGUST

Tie your painted shoes and dance,
blue daylight in your hair
Overhead a noiseless eagle fans a flame
Wonder everywhere

Garden parties are typically genteel affairs. The term 'garden party' alone calls up images of the aristocracy, properly dressed and coiffed, sipping tea and sampling petit fours while watching the children frolic about the green. Lawn croquet and shuttlecocks come to mind.

The Greenbank gang hosted a similar gathering each summer, their version a multi-cultural wingding of a jubilee. The lower branches of the yew were festooned, some anchoring balloons, some draped with streamers. Tables and chairs sat willy-nilly under the canopy.

The entire row-house turned out for the occasion, all twenty-two. Quite a rare occurrence these days. Some arrangements had to be made beforehand. Guests were invited. James and Sarah Doohan, along with the twins, May and June, attended. Everyone loved their dog, Myrtle,

Otter and Barky's mum, now eleven. James even brought Shankly, their foul-mouthed cockatoo.

Barky's original owners, Dennis 'Bones' Waters, his wife Donna and their daughters, Shannon and Cindy, were able to make it up from the Midlands. It was their financial plight, due to the stagnant building industry that forced the move from Liverpool, prompting Ben and Faith to adopt Barky.

Cyril and Luke had decided to invite Philip Carter. The meeting with Shea's family had piqued an interest already sparked with regards to the 'interpersonal dynamic' of the clan behind his two footballers. His wife, Harriet, came along with his son, Terence, and his two daughters, Gillian and Philippa.

"Please, call me Filly. Philippa is what you get when you're second born, not a boy, and your father's name is Philip."

"All right then, so it's Filly and Gilly?" asked Luke.

"To the end. Terry's the stuffy one, dad's protégé. He prefers Terence."

"Father got a son after all. All the pressure's on him." Gilly added. "Any of these children belong to you?"

"That blonde boy is Jacob. He's my son with Dani over there talking with your parents," Luke explained. "Ben here, and Faith, over there at the tables, are expecting in a few months."

"She's beautiful, Ben."

"That she is."

"I'll bet the baby will weigh a full stone," Filly said. "You two are large people!"

The four were down by the lake, watching the hounds swim. Lucas liked these girls; they had an edge about them. They looked to be in their early twenties, dressed nicely but in a counter-culture sort of way. Anti-posh, you might say.

Their brother was kicking a football around with Shea and the younger boys, trying to teach Jake and Gabe what a rondo was, them wanting to impress the older lads. Isaac was refereeing, Neff and James looking on.

"Neff old chap, what are we to do? It's like an Everton breeding ground round here."

"Aye, mate, but the Reds are back, we're winning trophies again!"

The Doohan twins and the Waters sisters were off picking wild-flowers for the table. Friends since primary school, the four were enjoying catching up with each other after nearly four years separation. Now the main subjects were boys, school, fashion, and boys. Shea and Terence had caught their eye, something their mothers noticed as well.

"Adolescence, it's not just for boys, you know."

"Amen, Sarah. Shannon's got a boyfriend. I think it's getting serious, but her eye still tends to wander. And Cynthia, well, only thirteen, but still."

"I hear ya, Donna, my two also. They act so sophisticated, but they won't give up their dolls."

Bones liked seeing his wife and her best friend together again. The Waters and Doohans had shared a lot through the years, being neighbors and raising their girls. Even Myrtle and her pups had become a part of their history.

Myrtle sat on the bank of the lake, watching her boys, getting an ear scratch from some nice young lady. Her muzzle was gray, her eyes not so clear anymore, but she was a happy dog, times like these were special.

Dani was checking Myrtle out. She'd been the old girl's vet her entire life. She was still in good health, suffering from only the normal effects of aging.

"A penny for your thoughts."

"Oh, hi Bashir. Just spacing out a bit. What's new? We haven't seen much of each other lately."

"I am thoroughly enjoying the end of my summer. Soon I'll have to start prepping for the new school year."

"You're going to lose one of your students this year."

"Oh yeah?"

"Uh-huh. Cyrus."

"That's right, we're passing him onto Lucas. I'll miss him, such a bright student and never a moment's trouble."

"Next year at this time you'll be bracing for Jake's scholastic debut."

"You mean a mini-Luke at Greenbank Primary? Allah, be merciful!"

"Hey you two." It was Robin and Colly. "We were thinking about bringing the food over."

"Good idea, I think everyone's ready."

"I'll get these tables put together," Bashir offered.

"I'll help you girls," Faith offered.

"Are you sure Faith, you've been a little under it of late."

"I'm fine. I can balance a dish on my belly."

"Groovy. Aleah, can you hold Poppy for a bit?"

"Absolutely!" She took the swaddled infant, cooing softly as she sat back down next to Hassan.

They were chatting with Philip and Harriet, the Ardavans not a lot older than the Carters.

"You've only left Iran this year?" Harriet asked.

"Yes, in February."

Philip was incredulous. "But the revolution was in full swing by then, the Shah had left."

"It was very bad then, utter chaos." Hassan explained. "Our son Cye, who's in the United States now, got out just in time."

"How were you permitted to leave?"

"We weren't. We had to be rescued."

"How, by who?"

"Lucas."

"Lucas Carter? Oh my word! How is that possible?"

"Luke lived in Iran. I was one of his teachers, Abbas his classmate. He speaks perfect Farsi," said Aleah.

Hassan continued, explaining the whole ordeal. The Carters were gobsmacked; Harriet had tears in her eyes.

"Amazing. If Lucas was English, he'd be knighted."

"You wouldn't hear it from him, but he's been the catalyst behind most of what's evolved here. He tempted Dani and Ben to come to Liverpool and he's known Cyril for twenty years."

"He can be cheeky. He referred to me as 'cuz' in our business meeting at Shea's signing. Apparently, he's a character with a lot of character."

"You never know what he'll come up with next. They are very close, those five, and very much dedicated to each other."

"Speak of the devil," said Hassan. Luke and Ben and the Carter sisters had walked back from the lake.

"Hey guys," he called to the footballers, "let's get cleaned up, soup's on."

"Lucas, I didn't know you'd lived in Iran. What work does your father do?"

"Construction. Yeah, we moved around a lot growing up."

"How many languages do you speak?"

"I'm still working on English."

Hassan smiled, "I told you, Philip."

"You know, football is becoming more global all the time. Players are emigrating to play in other countries. Maybe we could use a translator on our staff at Everton."

"Everton, squawk, Everton sucks!"

"What the hell?" the Carters looked up into the yew.

Ben was cracking up. "That's the Doohan's cockatoo, Shankly. James and Neff are Liverpool supporters." Gilly and Filly were much amused.

Luke helped Bashir with the tables and chairs while the Doohan and Waters girls went for jars and vases for their flowers. Then the platters, plates, and casseroles were carried over from the house. Everyone grabbed drinks and gathered under the yew.

It was a potluck affair, and there would be no dainty cups of tea and finger sandwiches for this lot. Instead, there was fried chicken and a ham, with coleslaw and macaroni salad, mixed fruit and spinach salad. Coolers were iced down with sodas, water, and ale. Iced tea was available, with homemade brownies and peanut butter cookies. Isaac, Barky, and Otter settled in for the long beg.

"Fried chicken is not a common dish here," Terence said to Cyril. "If it tasted as good as this, that would change."

"Colleen made it. She's from the south over in the States, in Florida."

"Didn't you say that's where your son Cye is, Hassan?" Philip asked.

"Yes, he's living with Ben's parents, in St. Petersburg. Kevin and Cheryl's oldest boy is there, as well."

"Really?" asked Harriet.

"Yes, Ian is a flutist, thanks to Abbas. He's in the symphony over there and going to University."

"Remarkable!"

"My sister Astrid stayed with them while she was in school too," Dani added. "They're wonderful people. Ben's father was the U.S. Ambassador to Great Britain in the '50s."

"Amazing! I'm starting to sense a pattern here," Philip said. "And that sign by the road, something about a Greenbank Coalition?"

"That's what some call our little collective here," Penny said, nodding towards her husband. "I thought at first he just wanted to be the landlord. Now, I'm convinced, he's set on world domination."

Bashir sat silent, a smug grin the only clue to his thoughts.

"Caaawk, sexy bird!"

"Oh, Aleah, I think Shankly fancies you," James said.

"Such a pretty bird," she replied. "And wise."

"Careful now, whoever's plate is directly below him."

"Eww, yuck!" declared Rose.

"This is quite the feast," Filly said between bites. "Best chicken ever!"

"Colly, let's open a restaurant. American style fried chicken with all the sides. We could call it 'Scouser Fried Chicken.'"

"Really, Cy? And who would be our spokesman? Colonel Sanders is taken."

"How about Shankly?"

"Finger lickin good, squawk!" was Ben's attempt at impersonation.

"Aaack, wanker!" was Shankly's reply.

"Tough crowd."

"That's one bawdy bird," Neff declared.

"I shouldn't let him watch football games," James admitted.

"Speaking of which, how's the squad shaping up ahead of the new campaign?" Kevin asked.

"On paper, very good," Philip reported. "Unfortunately, we can't play the games on paper. Gordon is enthused. The board has given him some new toys to play with. I'd say the outlook is bright. Cyril is in the changing room daily, has been for ten years. What's the verdict, Cy?"

"I would have to say guardedly good. There are quite a few new recruits, it will depend how quickly they get into the groove. I'm anxious to see that new young winger we brought up," he said, smiling at Shea.

"Here's to the people's club!"

"Up the Blues!"

Even James and Neff raised their glasses.

The sun was behind the trees on the other side of the lake by the time everyone had finished eating. The tables were cleared, the dogs seen to, and drinks freshened as the participants turned their chairs to face the sunset.

Abbas and Robin played their instruments, a mixture of tunes to soothe and relax. Only the Waters had left, wanting to cover the distance back down to the Midlands before dark. They seemed happy, adjusting to life in Lichfield, north of Birmingham. Bones thought the small town had a good family vibe.

"Wow, I just sorted it. Obs and Robs, the Eclectibles! I saw you and your band play Mountford Hall years ago. Unbelievably brilliant!" Gillian exclaimed.

"I remember," echoed Filly. "It's all you talked about for days."

"We haven't been able to get tickets since."

"We're putting a lineup together for the fall," said Robin. "We'll make sure you're there."

"Thank you, can't wait! What's the venue this time?"

"You'll have to ask our manager."

"Who's that?"

"Lucas."

"I might have known," Philip said with a resigned smile.

"Cooraawk! Rock on!"

CHAPTER 34
SUNDAY, 12 AUGUST

Take a walk down by,
take a walk down by the river
There's a lot that you,
there's a lot that you can learn
If you've got a mind that's open,
if you've got a heart that yearns

The cool, late summer morning broke fresh and clear, a slight breeze coming off the Mersey, the sun at their backs as they sat and watched the river flow towards the Irish Sea.

Cyril and Ben, along with their proteges, Seamus and Cyrus, had started out from Greenbank and run southeast, ending up at Otterspool Promenade, the public trail and green space occupying parts of the hamlets of Aigburth and Grassendale.

The elders had sensed some unease in the brothers. Both had big years ahead to look forward to, and knew that young boys, Shea in particular, tended to keep their misgivings bottled up.

"That was a pretty good pace you set getting down here Cy!" Cyril commented. "You been training on your own?"

"A bit. I've been running through Sefton Park in the mornings."

"Are you working towards something? Some kind of goal?"

"Surviving secondary school," Seamus cut in. "The older lads like to wind the new boys up."

"Ah, yeah, the good old days," Ben opined, "It happens everywhere, Cy. Something you gotta go through, like a gauntlet. You have to put up with it, to a certain extent. You also have to know when to draw the line. Don't let anyone embarrass or demean you. You may get beat up, but they'll learn to respect you."

"I've never been in a proper fight." The poor kid looked bewildered.

"The ones that will pick on you probably haven't either," Cyril said. "That's why they choose younger, smaller lads to bother. If you see it coming, and you know it's gonna happen, get the first shot in. Walk right up to the biggest one and punch him straight in the mouth. Make 'em all think twice. I promise you'll feel good about it. And don't worry, the birds love scars!"

"He's right, Cy," Ben agreed. "Last resort though, don't invite trouble. You can ignore their insults."

"How about your studies?" Cyril asked. "You know, after a while you'll get to choose some of your subjects."

"Well, that's got me confused as well. I love animals, helping Dani at the clinic is super. But I'm not good at science and maths. I don't want to disappoint her."

"Not a chance, kid, Dani loves you like her own, and you've been a big help to her. I don't get science much myself."

"Spot on," Ben agreed. "Her sister Astrid's the same, something about which part of your brain is more dominant."

"Dani and Astrid are not what I picture when I think of scientists."

"They make science sexy!" And that from the quiet one!

Cyril and Ben chuckled, "Right on Shea. Hell, there's nothing wrong with you guys. Don't worry, Cy, you can take your required subjects, your passions will surface as you go. How about you, Shea? This will be your last year, plus you've got a job. How's that for a balancing act?" Ben asked.

"Yeah, well, I've been getting loads of advice of late. I suppose I should be glad everyone cares, but I'm feeling pressure I didn't have before."

"Probably all of us older folks are guilty," Cyril admitted. "You're big news at home, Shea, we all want you to do well."

"We should remember you're typically soft-spoken, Shea, and you're uncomfortable in the spotlight. A bit like Cyril, really. He had to adjust to being celebrated, especially in public."

"Now they sing songs about him!"

"Wanna know my secret?"

"Please, not that I'll ever be as famous."

"You've got all you need, soft lad, just takes time. Anyway, you need your own 'Mona Lisa' smile."

"What's that?"

"Your go-to public countenance. A slight grin, bemused-like, to keep 'em guessing. Say as little as possible, let them fill in the blanks and wonder later where they got it wrong."

"Corr! Where did you learn that, back in Trinidad from your da?"

"No, from Lucas."

"You both can lean on Luke this year," Ben advised. "He can teach you things you can't learn in the classroom, or on the pitch."

"You know what?" Cyrus informed. "That's almost exactly what Ian said when he left for America."

"Ian was even younger than you are now when your family moved in," Cyril said. "He was captivated by all of us strange foreigners."

"I miss him," Shea sighed. "I hope he comes back, at least for a visit, sometime soon."

"He's kicking ass, apparently, doing really well. Maybe he'll get time in the fall to come over."

"Maybe mum and da will go to Florida," mused Cy. "I don't think they've ever had holidays, maybe when they first got married."

"That's something Cy and I have talked about. Our parents are in a rut," agreed Shea.

"And now that Ian and Shea have jobs, I'm their only burden. They should do a proper vacation."

Ben and Cyril had a chuckle.

"A burden you are, eh?"

"Could the chippy stay open while they're gone?" Ben asked.

"Easily!" Shea said. "We've a good manager in Gloria, Da trusts her. He'd have to order in extra supplies before they left. There's plenty of help, business is a bit off and the staff want all the hours they can get."

"I imagine you lads are right, and good on you, thinking of your folks like that. Tell you what, Ben and I will talk it over with the rest. I bet we can sort it."

"Do you guys think they'd agree to it? Maybe we can surprise them."

"Yes, arrange it in advance, make it hard to say no," Shea agreed.

"Done!" Ben declared. "Okay, let's head back, see what's happening at the old homestead."

Cyrus and Seamus set the pace, spirits buoyed by the unburdening of their souls and a glimpse of the future. The older 'boys' brought up the rear.

"Well done, Cy. You've got a fatherly side, you know."

"Shush, me brother, it's our secret. You sure you should've compared school to a gauntlet?"

"Yeah. It is, in a way. At least I didn't tell them to grin like a girl."

CHAPTER 35
MONDAY, 27 AUGUST

A thought of colored clouds all high above my head
A trip that doesn't need a ticket or a bed

Ben was having a multi-sensory overload. Bright, flashing colors, rhythmic, pulsating music, and sensuous, heated movements, all enveloping, totally dominating the here and now.

No, he wasn't tripping, or part of an orgy. He was at a carnival in Leeds. Not Rio, not Port of Spain. Leeds.

And, he was getting paid. The Echo had sent him to cover the event, the thirteenth edition of the Leeds West Indian Carnival, the oldest Caribbean themed festival in Europe.

It was a four-day affair, culminating on the last Monday of August, a bank holiday throughout Great Britain.

He'd come to the west of Yorkshire on the train, just seventy miles northeast of Liverpool, skirting Manchester on the way. The paper had booked a room in the City Centre for him, the area known mainly for its football team, and Leeds University.

Carnival kicked off on Friday with the Queen's show. The Queens were the leaders of their particular troupes and had the biggest and most elaborate costumes. Judges choose the best while surrounded by steel bands and dancers.

Saturday is marked by the Calypso Monarch contest, a competition for aspiring musicians and Calypso singers. It turned out to be Ben's favorite part of the long weekend; people slowed down enough to be talked to and photographed. He was buoyed by the spirit of these people possessing a positive, forward-looking approach to life, their way of thumbing their noses at the past. Carnival had its roots in slavery, and was a celebration of its adherent's refusal to accept such bondage as their lot in life.

Two of the carnival's original organizers, Arthur France and Ian Charles, were generous with their time, always willing to further the cause, as were most everyone he encountered. He even scored a quote from the newly chosen carnival queen.

Sunday brought a less structured agenda to the fest. Ben visited the street vendors, checked out some guys making pan drums, and managed to survive partying with a group of Jamaicans. He hit the sack early, buzzed and tired. Monday was the big day.

It started with J'ouvert, which meant 'daybreak' in French patois. J'ouvert is an early morning parade, something to stir up folks, set the mood for the day. Many people embraced the custom of coming in pajamas or onesies, freedom of expression on full display.

The big event, the main parade, began at two, setting off from the staging area within Potternewtown Park. It was about a seven-mile route to the City Centre and back.

At present Ben was anchored in place at the corner of Chapeltown Road and Francis Street, a neighborhood of Edwardian terraces. He had a high vantage point, sitting on a large boulder outside the Roscoe Methodist Church. The sun was at his back, the oncoming parade being picked off one shutter click at a time. He was glad he'd brought a lot of film.

"Hello, journo mon!"

"Hey, fellas. What's happening?" Two young dudes, students probably, were smiling up at him. He jumped off his perch and introduced himself.

"Pleased to meet you. I am Henry Fountain, dis here is Samuel Kennedy. We noticed your press pass. You are from Liverpool?"

"Yes sir, and you?"

"We live here, in Leeds. But we're both Trinis, from Port of Spain. We were wondering, since you are a newspaper mon, if you might be acquainted with de Everton footballer, Cyril Barcant?"

"Yes, I know him personally. Quite the player, he is."

"For true!" Samuel exclaimed. "He cuts a big figure back home, took us to de World Cup!"

"We were at Elland Road last Wednesday when Everton played Leeds United," Henry added. "Masterful!"

"Here, let me take your picture. I'll let Cyril know he's got fans in Yorkshire."

"Tank you!" Samuel gushed, "I'm probably four or five years younger but I saw Cyril play for Maple in Port of Spain many years ago."

"Wow, small world!"

"Gettin more so every dey!"

"So, Mister Ben, will you be stayin for the fete dis evening?"

"I wish. No, I need to hop a train for Merseyside in a bit. Probably for the best. All this celebration is taking a toll."

"Come na, big mon, all you need is practice!"

"I don't know guys, the jerk, the rum, and the scotch bonnets are barking at me."

"Fete for so!"

CHAPTER 36
WEDNESDAY, 29 AUGUST

We're the kings of Goodison, we play in Royal Blue,
The home of all the Toffeemen, we play it sweet for you

Everton's season had started poorly. Manager Gordon Lee's chop and change of the club's roster over the summer was evident in the disjointed performances thus far. Tonight's match would afford a chance to put things right, due to the nature of the competition. It was the first cup game of the campaign.

European football clubs had the potential to play in four different competitions during the year. Besides the regular season, there were two domestic cup tournaments, and, if you were good enough to qualify, the European Cup was up for grabs. In England, the two domestic cups were the League Cup and the Football Association Cup, the oldest footballing competition in the world.

Tonight, Everton was hosting Cardiff City in the League Cup. The Bluebirds, from the Welsh capital, had made the long trip up from the shore of Bristol Bay for the seven-thirty kickoff.

Just a block away from the stadium gates a contingent from Greenbank had joined the Mason brothers at the Abbey, their usual pre-game watering hole.

The gang now had seven tickets to every home match. Cyril's normal allotment was four, Seamus', somehow, was three, one more than was customary for a rookie. Lucas strikes again. This evening it was Penny, Bashir, Robin, and Abbas joining the McTimons.

"Six Guinnesses and a coke, please, John."

"Straight away, Clive. Quite the crew you've got."

"Yeah mate, we've a new recruit on the club, a junior the Blues brought up."

"Is that right? Which one?"

"The eleven, McTimons."

"I've heard of him. A bright lad, they say."

"We'll see."

A gorgeous sky cast its glow on Walton Lane thirty minutes before kickoff, a scarf and a pint the only extra warmth necessary against the chill of the late summer's eve. Cyrus led the procession, wearing his brother's shirt proudly. Both Penny and Robin were sporting the number six, Barcant on the back.

The pregame rituals, warm-ups, and announcements were conducted, the supporters ramping up the atmosphere and, finally, the referee initiated the proceedings.

The visitors, underdogs on paper, started conservatively, trying to keep their shape defensively in a 4-4-2 formation. They had some dangerous players, capable of hurting Everton on the counter.

The gaffer had tinkered with the lineup at the start of the season, resulting in inconsistent performances. As a central midfielder, Cyril was in a position to affect this problem. He played in a triangle, slightly behind Asa Hartford and Trevor Ross, leaving Andy King out on the wing. Asa was the new guy in midfield, but the Scot brought some good experience to the side, having played in last year's World Cup. Brian Kidd and the skipper, Cy's mate Mick Lyons, were the forwards. Mick used to come forward late in games when the Toffees needed a goal, the manager starting the big man up front tonight to give the team a focal point in attack.

Everton had the majority of possession, the breakthrough coming in the twenty-sixth minute. Cy had won the second ball off a long cross defended by Billy Wright in his own box and passed the ball up to Mick, showing at about thirty-five yards from goal. He trapped, then turned and slotted a streaking Kidd through the back line, chipping the keeper for the opening goal. Goodison erupted. Mick winked at the away supporters in the Park End Stand.

Cardiff tried to respond, pushing forward, trying to work the wings, but to no avail. Everton's midfield triangle shifted as needed, cutting off service to their forwards.

Halftime came, trips to the loo, and chatting with the neighbors. 'Moneypenny' was there in the players section, grooving on Mick's assist.

"Oh, for heaven's sake, Pat!" Penny was elated at seeing Pat and Brian LaBone. 'Labby' was an Everton icon, captain of the team when Cyril first played. Pat had made the gang feel welcome from the first match, and had confided to Penny that the couple were trying to get pregnant. Penny had just given birth to Rose that year and the two had bonded. Now their daughter, Rachelle, was nine years old.

Brian huddled with the McTimons, wanting to get to know the new kid's family. "He's an up and comer. I didn't realize he grew up next to Cyril. That's a plus, and he's obviously from good stock" making Cheryl blush. "I had that crazy West Indian as the first name on the team sheet one day. Now I suspect Seamus won't be far behind." Kevin was starstruck, LaBone was a legend.

Cardiff City came out in the second half determined to give a better account of themselves. This meant playing a lot of long balls and being more aggressive. The Blues sat back a bit, absorbing the early pressure. Gordon decided to change tactics to neutralize the visitor's efforts.

Football fans love it when one of the local lads finds his way onto the first team, so it was no surprise to see Seamus McTimons warmly welcomed onto the pitch in the fifty-eighth minute. Andy King was feeling his hamstring tighten, Shea his natural replacement.

He was nervous, cup competitions were important to everyone. He leaned over, snatched a blade of grass, and put it in his mouth. He then took his first step on the storied pitch.

All nervousness was gone two minutes later when he collected a pass from the defense and started up the right wing. Billy Ronson, Cardiff's left mid, ran twenty yards and delivered a two-footed sliding tackle, missing the ball completely and sending Shea off the pitch into the advert boards.

Luckily, Mick got there before Cyril. The fans roared, wanting justice, the perp getting off with just a yellow card.

Shea popped right up, checked himself for damage, and jogged back onto the field, smiling at Ronson. "That all ya got?" Cy smiled and the fans cheered, Kevin and Cheryl were able to breathe again.

The match settled down some afterwards, becoming more of a cat and mouse affair. Then, suddenly, Cyril picked off a pass at midfield, and found Trevor Ross on the left. Trevor sidestepped a challenge and sent a long, cross-field diagonal pass to a streaking Shea on the right flank, who blew by their fullback and sent a low screamer infield to Mick, on the corner of the penalty box. Mick dummied, letting the ball nutmeg him and roll onto Brian Kidd's instep drive, bulging the back of the net at the Gwladys Street End.

The din was sudden and overwhelming, a cacophony of joyful noise. Mick and Brian waited for Shea, embracing him between them and presenting him to the adoring crowd.

Still, the Bluebirds of Wales, to their credit, did not throw in the towel. Everton dropped into their game management shape, leaving only Shea and Brian as outlets. Shea was a pest, harassing Cardiff with his pace and tenacity. Another crunching tackle, this time by Alan Campbell on Shea, saw both Campbell and Trevor Ross getting booked. The Toffees took care of their own.

The full-time whistle was accompanied by chants and cheers, the faithful spilling out into the streets, giddily reliving their heroes' exploits. A group walking behind the gang on the way to the car park were lauding the new kid.

"They'll be singing songs about that new lad, McTimons, afore long. A sensation, he is."

CHAPTER 37
SATURDAY, 1 SEPTEMBER

The peasants celebrate with song and dance
The joy of a rich harvest

The Liverpool Philharmonic Hall was one of the city's crown jewels. Home of the Royal Liverpool Philharmonic Society, the acoustically pure venue held events for the orchestra, the youth orchestra, the chamber music ensemble, and its various choirs.

The art-deco structure, opened in '39, sat on Hope Street, halfway between the Catholic and Anglican cathedrals. Constructed of fawn colored facing bricks, the front featured semi-circular stair turrets at both corners, and a canopied entrance. Above the entrance were seven pier-spaced windows, topped with carved abstract motifs.

John and Sylvie Quinn were at Neff's house, chatting with Hassan and Aleah and playing with their grandson and the kittens. The four of them had tickets to the symphony this evening, always excited at the chance to see their kids perform.

"Gabriel is such a joy," Sylvie cooed, sitting on the floor with a set of Lincoln Logs. "I wish we had more time together."

"I should start bringing him round the market," Aleah offered. "Children grow up much too fast!"

"I say! Such visions of beauty, heaven on earth!"

"Hello Neff, where have you been all day?" Hassan inquired.

"In the Wirral. Purely a reconnaissance mission. I haven't been to the other side of the Mersey in ages." He looked around, assaying the scene. "What's on? Such a turned-out lot, you are."

"We're headed for the Phil," replied John, "to mingle with the gentry."

"Ah, an evening of culture. Take care your offspring don't go Obs and Robs!"

"Obs and Robs?" Sylvie asked on the way up Hope Street.

Hassan chuckled, "That's their alter-egos, in the Eclectibles. Cyril came up with it."

"Catchy."

Abbas and Robin were presently backstage, preparing for tonight's performance. The mood was light, but edgy. Four works were on the slate, not a long program, but challenging.

The symphony's principal conductor, Walter Weller, was in his third year at the Society's helm. The Austrian violinist, about to turn forty, did not possess much in the way of flamboyance, and was not particularly ambitious, like so many of his peers. Born in Vienna, he was rooted in the richly textured, string based Viennese style, even placing the first and second violins together on his left with cellos and basses on the right. This suited Robin just fine. She had grown under his tutelage, refining her craft in ways she hadn't pondered before. He loved her fire and spirit, but she had to learn when to unleash it, and when to let it sit and simmer.

"The notes are important; take care to honor the space between the notes as well," he had told her.

The interior of the venue was gorgeous, narrowing from the back of the balcony to the stage, with sensuously curved walls on the sides, adorned with incised female figures suggesting different musical moods.

The hall started to fill up, both patrons and musicians, an anticipatory air building, waiting for the man.

The man was all business, perfunctorily acknowledging the applause while striding to the rostrum and taking up his baton.

Vivaldi's Four Seasons, consisting of four violin concertos, was one of the first works to feature a narrative element, the instruments portraying parts of the story. Vivaldi even wrote four accompanying sonnets, supplementary to the score.

Autumn was chosen for tonight's performance, a nod to the calendar, its three movements describing the harvest and its subsequent celebrations, along with preparations for the hunt. Walter was pleased, his charges had hit the ground running.

He then led them into Danses Concertantes, Igor Stravinsky's controversial composition for chamber orchestra. Fluid and lively, it was a joy to perform. Written in 1942, post-war students complained that the piece was too old-fashioned. Well, Iggy was a neo-classicist, the young whelps would have to get over themselves. A work in five movements, Stravinsky's experimentation in meter, rhythm, and tonality did spark the imagination, the man was more rebel than old fogey.

The second half of the concert was all Mozart. Wolfgang, and his father, Leopold, had left Italy all those years ago for Mannheim, hoping to catch on in the city known for its orchestra, and the generosity of its patrons. While not initially successful, he did get a commission to write three concertos and two quartets for flute.

Poor Wolfi fell in love, with Aloisia Weber, sister of his future wife Constanze, and only completed one concerto.

The flute concerto in G major had an opening allegro that featured some sonatic elements, leading to the Adagio, with its more peaceful caress. The final movement, the Rondo, was coy, tempering virtuosic heat with echoes of the opening melody.

While dealing with events in Mannheim, Mozart's friend back home in Salzburg, Sigmund Haffner, had been promoted to the nobility. To celebrate his compatriot and honor the occasion, he composed one of his grandest works, symphony number thirty-five, the 'Haffner', in D major.

The orchestra rolled up its sleeves and dove right in. The Allegro con Spirito was just that, powerful and dramatic, with striking contrasts between the winds and strings. Abbas and Robin, the yin and yang.

The Andante, typically a more lyrical follow up, still carried majestic leanings. And the Menuetto, even it had a sturdiness not normally felt in third movements.

The final movement, Presto, brought back the pace and emotion of the first, albeit more concise; a rushing, dazzling finale.

Mozart had intended the symphony to be played as fast as possible, while maintaining clarity. The last note's echoes found everyone in the hall trying to catch their breath. Bravo!

Chapter 38
Friday, 14 September

Official moments of the guild
in poses keen from bygone days
City fathers frozen there
upon the canvas dark with age

Neff felt it before he heard it. Vibration, very subtle, but very near. In the bed with him, he realized, his eyes popping open as the sound of the vibration registered in the here and now. Behind him, on top of the covers, in the crook formed by his bended knees, Div slept, purring contentedly. Typical. Neff had a way with the youngsters.

He padded over to the bathroom to drain the water off the potatoes, taking stock in the mirror while washing up afterwards. Today was his seventy-fifth birthday.

"Serviceable," he whispered to himself. His frame still erect, his eyes clear and blue as ever, and he still had his hair, never mind that it was nearly white.

Donning socks, slippers, and a housecoat, he and the little gray tabby made their way into the kitchen to start a pot of water.

Signs of life were emanating from the upstairs, Hassan and Aleah beginning their day. Pari appeared from parts unknown, mewling her desire for breakfast. Neff obliged as Div joined the chorus.

The weather was agreeable, so he retrieved the morning's edition of the Echo from the front stoop and went to the back garden with his cup of tea and a shortbread, surprising Ben, who was doing God knows what, out between the shed and the firepit.

"Busted!"

"Indeed. Out with it, lad."

"Here, give me a hand."

It turned out to be a banner, of sorts. A swath of white cloth, probably bed linen, about two feet wide and six feet long, each end attached to a pair of two-by-two pine posts.

"Happy Birthday, partner!"

Big block letters were hand painted along the banner's length. 'Happy Burfday, Baba' the message. Caspar was the author. The other children had provided accompanying artwork; colorful images such as dogs, footballs, party hats, and balloons.

"The secret is out, me thinks."

"Roll with it, Neff. You're quite popular round here."

Once installed, they confirmed it to be square, level, and plumb. Ben went inside to get a cup of tea of his own.

He returned, Aleah in tow, the aroma of strong coffee in her cup. "I remember when I was teaching at the American School in Tehran, every morning the smell of coffee. Hassan and I got hooked, though we do still enjoy a cup of tea. Happy Birthday, Neff," she said, kissing him on the cheek.

"Thank you, my dear."

The gate on the north side of the garden opened, admitting nearly two hundred and thirty pounds of English Otterhound, and about one hundred and seventy pounds of Aleah's Persian progeny.

"Good morning, son."

"Subh bakheer, Mather. And happy birthday, Neff!"

"Thank you, Abbas. Cup of tea?"

"No, sir, I've got to take Otter home and feed Barky. They're thirsty, too. Just wanted to pop in for a bit."

"Barky no!" He had hiked his leg on one of the banner posts.

"Ah, an art critic," mused Ben.

"I was an art teacher," Aleah interjected. "I think it's brilliant!"

Otter was eyeing Neff's biscuit.

"Come on, you two. I get the hint." The hounds followed Abbas back through the gate.

The gate on the south side opened as the other closed. "I thought I heard voices."

"Morning, Penny. Isaac, what's up little guy?"

"Good morning, Benjamin. Happy Birthday, Neff!" Birthday boy got his second buss of the day. "Aleah, is that coffee I smell?"

"It is. Let me get you a cup."

"Got it," Hassan said, about to come out the back door.

Soon the four were seated, facing the rising sun, about to show itself over the roofs of the rowhouses to the east.

"Well, Neff, what's on today. Any plans?" asked Penny.

"It's a big one, Baba," informed Hassan.

"Seventy-five. I believe that's called a platinum jubilee?" asked Ben.

"Yes," Neff replied. "I find, however, this platinum a bit rusty."

"Nonsense!" corrected Penny, "Hale and hardy, you are." Isaac yipped in agreement.

"There you are!" It was Cyril and Seamus. "Happy Birthday, Neff!" they said in unison.

"Thanks lads. You off to training?"

"Yes, then on the coach, bound for Ipswich," Cy explained. "We've a match with the Blues tomorrow."

"That's a long trip," Penny remarked.

"They're called the Blues, as well?" asked Neff.

"Yeah, or the Tractor Boys," said Shea.

"That's Suffolk for ya."

"A good side, now that Bobby Robson's the gaffer," Cy said.

"Have a good trip, lads. Thanks for the birthday wishes."

"We could probably get you on the supporter's coach. We know you're a Toffees lover now," Cy teased.

"Go on, off with you now, ya blue buggers!"

"Why don't you gentlemen enjoy the morning while I fix breakfast. Penny, can I tempt you to stay?"

"Easily, luv. But I've got to get my lot off to school."

"And I've got to be at the office within the hour," Ben said.

"Okay, you two, what would you like?"

"Neff?" Hassan said. "Your choice."

"Porridge and toast, please."

"That's all? Nothing special?"

"No, thank you. I've a lunch date."

The rest of the morning was spent in a relaxed manner with those that didn't have to go out to pursue their livelihoods, or a higher education.

It was a short list today, even Penny was going into the pharmacy for a half day. Also, Hassan was going with George Stillwell to check out an old railway station for a four-home complex.

That left Aleah, Cheryl, Gabe, Jake, and Poppy. The telly, and a read-along with Aesop, was followed by an hour in the park with Isaac and Otter.

Neff's lunch date was at the request of a former professor at the Liverpool College of Art, Julia Preston Carter.

Julia was a museum quality potter, from a local family of celebrated artists. Her great gran, for whom art was just a hobby, was Lord Mayor of Liverpool in the 1850s. Her father, who was the Anglican Cathedral's chief sculptor, was a designer of coins and medals. Her brother was also a sculptor, her mother a watercolor artist.

She left her teaching position just a few years earlier to focus on her art, and was fast becoming the leading ceramicist in the distinctive sgraffito style of etching designs into clay.

Neff had met Julia in the mid-sixties when she turned up at his office looking for some historical perspective on which to base a current project. They'd discovered a mutual appreciation for each other's chosen field of endeavor, and remained friends ever since. She was aware of his birthday and offered to spring for lunch.

They met at the Ship and Mitre on Dale Street. Neff paused in the building's foyer, gazing at the plaque referencing the site's beginnings as a coach house in the last century.

"I thought you knew all this by heart?" she said, surprising him with his third kiss on the cheek of the day.

"Julia, my dear, so good to see you, as bright and lovely as ever!" He took her hand. "How long has it been?"

"Ages, luv, much too long."

"Come, let's sit."

They took a table in the downstairs pub and ordered a pint while perusing the menu.

"Cheers!"

"Happy Birthday! The pub looks different to me somehow."

"Yes, they've gradually changed the décor down here over the past five or six years."

"Looks like the inside of a ship."

"That's the idea. The upstairs is relatively unchanged, art deco primarily."

"Mister History. Okay, when was the pub opened?"

"Mid-thirties. It was called The Flagship, then the Mitre, finally combined to Ship and Mitre."

"Sharp as ever, you are."

They each had a salad and shared a sandwich and friendly banter, catching up with each other's lives' latest.

"Your work is amazing, Julia. And it's turning up in more and more prestigious galleries. You've been busy."

"I have. And I do miss teaching, seeing the inspiration in those eager young eyes. But it's better for me, to be able to focus solely on my craft. We should be able to chat more often now, that's a plus."

"Actually, I'm reminded of you more than you're aware."

"Oh, how so?"

"When I visit the Anglican Cathedral," he said with a twinkle in his eye. She visibly reddened.

"I shall never live this down! How did you find out?"

"Your father. We were there as a coincidence. He couldn't help himself."

Her father, Edward, had sculpted the Nativity at the Cathedral. The baby Jesus looked like the infant Julia's twin brother.

"At least I was a baby then. No one will know it now unless dad blabs it about."

"Immortalized in stone."

"Poppycock!"

After lunch they walked east on Dale, negotiated the roundabout, and continued on William Brown Street, past the World Museum complex to the Walker Art Gallery. Neff was the gallery tour guide, Julia the authority on its contents.

It was opened in September of 1877, financed by Andrew Barclay Walker, a brewer and city alderman. He was not a patron of the arts and confessed to not knowing much about the subject. He was, however, a wealthy and generous man, erecting an assortment of public houses in the city. The Walker Art Gallery displayed classic works in different forms dating back to the 12th century. Julia's knowledge and appreciation of the myriad of disciplines shown was impressive and stimulating.

They parted with a promise to keep in touch more often. Today had been a treat. He saw her to the bus stop on the way to the car park.

"I shall expect to see your work at the Walker soon enough."

"And I shall expect you, should my father be tempted to spill the family secrets, to tell him to stuff a sock in his gob!"

Neff pulled to the curb at Greenbank, Ben had given him the Traveler for the day. It was late afternoon, he wanted to bathe, and maybe even read today's paper.

He did get the shower; the rest was not to be. The banner was now adorned with real balloons, a bunch tethered to each post. The fire pit was readied, chairs were scattered about, and one table was covered with wrapped gifts and a huge carrot cake with seven and a half candles.

"Busted!" Ben said.

CHAPTER 39
WEDNESDAY, 26 SEPTEMBER

Mama-yo
I start to dance
I start to prance
Because the buzzin' of the bee
Form this beautiful melody

Cheryl was dancing with Allan Joseph to calypso music, the lyrics difficult to understand, something about nasty bees and jumping about. The instrumentation was strange and exotic, yet seductive, making it easy to 'shake a tail feather.'

Kevin was deep in conversation with Wayne and Chris Tucker, getting the scoop on Cyril and Luke's childhood together. He was dressed in a Panama shirt and khaki shorts. And sandals. Yes, sandals, exposing his toes to the world for the first time since he was a child.

Michael and Allison Barcant were giddy, just watching their two English friends enjoying themselves. The past nine days had seen the pair touring in and around Port of Spain, and, more importantly, getting to know each other. The Barcants had been to Liverpool a handful of times over the past ten years, and they'd gradually gotten better acquainted with the McTimons during that time. But going to Liverpool meant being with the gang. It was exhausting. In contrast, the time spent here with the McTimons had cemented the relationship. Michael cherished their simple, honest, salt of the earth mentality, Allison their commitment to friends and family. Cheryl and Kevin truly loved Cyril and the way he and his bunch had inspired their sons.

Allison had suggested tonight's open house potluck affair as a way for the McTimons to meet their friends and neighbors. She was intrigued, in an almost mischievous way, by mixing up the guest list in social settings. It often resulted in the most interesting conversations.

Kevin kept close to the food, nibbling here and there, a rum and coke at the ready.

"What you tink, mistah Kevin, you like the mango chow?" asked Gally Cummings.

"Is that what it's called? It's the strangest thing I've ever tasted." He took another bite. "But I can't stop."

Gally laughed, "I've been keeping my eye on your club, by the way. Their fortunes seem to rise and fall but Cyril is still a real force of nature."

"That he is. First name on the team sheet. How about you, Gally? Where are you these days?"

"Freshly retired. I played some indoors in the States this year but it's not for me. I had some good years up there in the NASL and in Mexico but I'm thirty-one now and have lost more than a step."

"I thought you were one of the stars of the national team back in Germany. A real handful you were, lad."

"Tank you, that was a time, eh?"

"Brilliant!"

"Hey, you two, out de way. I need some more nourishment."

"You're always hungry, Allan."

"Hey, dancing with Lady Cheryl takes energy, don't ya know. Kevin, mon, she's a natural, great rhythm."

"She didn't learn it from me."

"Ah, here we go, chicken and rice."

"Careful Allan," warned Kevin. "That one's hot!"

"That's de scotch bonnet."

"I can tell ya nothing in Scotland is that hot."

"So, Kevin, tell us more about Seamus. You must be the proud papa, no?"

"Don't get him started!" chided Cheryl, eyeing the buffet. "He'll talk himself silly."

Allan and Cheryl filled their plates and went over to sit with the Tucker brothers' parents, Glenn and Sheelah. They had been good friends with the Carters when they lived in Trinidad.

And, speaking of Seamus, Catherine and her roomie had just arrived, Cat wearing the Everton number eleven.

"Wow, nice party!"

"Fete for so!" Kevin replied, in his best island lilt.

"There ya go! Kevin, I'd like you meet Millicent Hathaway. Millie, this is Kevin McTimons, one of my favorite people ever, and father to three very studly young men.

"Millie, hello. I'm so glad we could meet. Catty's told us so much about you."

"Pleased to meet you, Kevin," she said, kissing his cheek. "I was going to say the same exact thing."

"Nice shirt, Catty."

"Yes, thanks so much. Fits well, don't you think?"

"Perfect! It looks better on you than Shea."

Over at a table by the terrace the senior Tuckers were quizzing Cheryl about Luke.

"So little Lucas is a teacher now?" Sheelah asked.

"Yes, at secondary school nearby our house. He teaches languages, French and Spanish."

"I used to drive a carload of children to school each morning. Lucas and Wayne are the same age. I remember he had our Trini accent down like a native in no time at all," Glenn said.

"What caused you to decide to come to Trinidad for holidays?"

"Oh, Sheelah, we didn't really have a choice. Our sons sorted it on their own and just popped up one day with the tickets. Catherine arranged it at her travel firm, and Allison and Michael have been so generous and kind."

"Well, I hope you've been enjoying your stay."

"It's been paradise!" Kevin said, joining the conversation. "We've really not traveled at all before this, but I can't imagine a better place to visit."

While Kevin entertained the Tuckers with his boy-like awe of Trinidad, Cheryl went to freshen her drink. She also wanted to chat with Catherine and meet Millie. She found them at the edge of the terrace, enjoying the view.

"Cheryl! Join us, this is Millie."

"Finally!" They shared an embrace. "Such a vision you are, lass." That she was. Tall, fit looking, short blond hair.

"I've been looking forward to meeting you too, Cheryl. How's your stay here been?"

"The best! Look at this view, all the way to the sea. And Allison's house, like out of a dream! The way it's built into the side of the hill. And on this side, no windows, just open to the heavens!"

"We have very few problems with insects, and the weather, so close to the equator, it's very steady," Millie explained.

"I'm glad we have you to ourselves, Cheryl. I'd like to ask your advice about Cyril." Cat seemed worried.

"Of course, luv, is it about the two of you?"

"Yes, I don't know how to tell him." The poor girl suddenly seemed on the verge of tears.

"Nonsense! You came out to your parents, did you not?"

"Yes. Well, I told mum. She told dad."

"And how did he react?"

"Remarkably well. I think he actually was hurt I didn't come to him myself."

"Well then, I would think Cyril wouldn't want to hear it from anyone else as well."

"Yeah, I guess I know that. It's just, I don't know, I don't want him to somehow be disappointed."

"Again, nonsense! Cy's a full-grown man now. And despite that macho, warrior thing he's got going on, he's one of the kindest souls on earth. He loves you like mad, that's for sure. Knowing Cyril, he'd probably, if he wasn't married, try to talk this lovely lady into changing her tune, so to speak." Both girls laughed.

"Thanks, Cheryl. You're very wise. I feel so much better," giving her a hug. "I did meet Colleen, at Luke and Dani's reception. Cy was showing interest in her then, I think. She's very attractive, I ought to know, right?" They all laughed at that one.

"You should come for a visit, the both of you. You can talk to your brother, show him how happy you are."

"Whoa, that would be so cool!"

"We have been thinking of getting away together," Millie said.

"You could stay with us," Cheryl offered. "Ian's with Ben's folks in Florida and Shea's gone half the time. I'd love it!"

"Super! I would have wondered where to stay; that bunch are having babies like rabbits! Oh, Millie, it will be cold there, we can bundle up!"

"I'm not sure that's a reason to get excited, but sure, come this fall or winter," Cheryl reasoned.

"Such a kind invitation, Cheryl, I'd love to go. I've heard so much about your families and Liverpool. We could see your son and Cyril play football!"

Directly below the three conspirators, out on the sloped back lawn, Michael, Gally, Kevin, and Allan were talking football, business, and rum.

"Never had it before last week," Kevin reported. "Very smooth."

"Tankfully produced now without the need for slaves," Allan pointed out.

"Amen, "said Michael. "The colonial days are behind us now."

"For true," Gally agreed. "Class distinctions still exist but educated blacks and whites have come together."

"We've struggled with this in Liverpool of late. Our port has seen tens of thousands of slaves come through the docks. We've named streets and parks after those involved in slave trading and now many are feeling disappointment and shame."

"We all live and learn," mused Allan. "It's sad when de next generation doesn't pay heed."

"Well said my friend."

"Cheers to that!" They all raised their glasses.

"Hey, down there, what's all the yakking bout?" It was Pat Fojo, the Barcant's neighbor.

"Solving the world's problems. We've nearly got it figured out," Michael reported.

Now Allison, Cheryl, and the girls were looking over the balcony.

"So, what's the solution?" Millie asked.

"More rum, less slaves."

"Brilliant!"

"By the way, Michael, what's this?" Kevin was looking at the door nearby on the lower level.

"Maid's quarters."

Allan and Gally could not contain themselves.

"Not to worry, this is not a plantation. Eileen lived here back in the day. Allison and I were both working, and the children were in school. Eileen had three kids and no husband. She was nineteen years old. So, her mother saw to the children during the week, and she lived here and kept house and went home on the weekend. Then we paid for her to attend college and get her and her family back on track."

"And she's married, to one of our old football mates," Gally said. "Great fellow, adores the children."

"It's nice to hear stories like that."

"So, Kevin, tomorrow's our last day in Eden. Cat wants to know what's on?"

"How about Maracas Bay?"

"Kev, we've been twice; you nearly drowned!"

"Nah, I'm only getting better. I was born to ride the wild surf!" Cowabunga!

TRIBUTE

CHAPTER 40
SATURDAY, 29 SEPTEMBER

Shall I play for you
pa rum pum pum pum
On my drum

I t started with an index card, thumb tacked to a message board, in a pub that featured live music:

```
Drummer seeks band
Multi-genre grooves
Improvisational attitudes
Call George 051-362-4239
```

Well, that sounded interesting. Luke copied down the info and rang George up on Thursday. George was a yank. He said he moved over the pond from Florida, but Luke pegged him as being from the upper eastern seaboard. They agreed to meet and yak it up.

As he entered the Bramley-Moore he was thinking this may be the oldest pub he'd ever been to, including James Doohan's Baltic Fleet. It was adjacent to Bramley Moore dock on what used to be the old Dock Road, north of Pier Head, almost to Bootle, where George said he worked.

The interior was a bit drab but had some cool old stuff. Nothing fancy, chilled ales and hot food.

"Mr. Carter, I presume?"

"Mr. Pearson, nice to meet you. How's things?"

"Splendid! I just got off work for the weekend a couple of hours ago."

"Yeah, where's that?"

"Sattie's, or Satterthwaite's, I should say. I'm a baker."

"No kidding?"

"Yeah, here, I got us a table." They sat over by a window. "And here's a bag of barm cakes for you. I'm digging baking British style, but all the nomenclature takes some getting used to."

"Thanks! Yeah, you'd think they could just say dinner roll. I've heard of Sattie's, but they're all up here or further north. I'm down near Sefton Park."

"Nice area. I live not far from here, in a flat by Canada Dock. Basic, but there's an attached workshop that's been cleared out that my kit is set up in. It's great. I work from four til ten or eleven then I can clean up, grab a bite and practice."

"I'll bet bedtime comes early. You sure you have time for gigs?"

He smiled, "You bet! Name the place and time."

"Cool. Look, you're gonna need to keep your day job. This band is a collective. They practice, if you can call it that, at Dovedale Towers every week or so, whoever can show up at the time. No one gets paid, you get free pints and a share of the tip jar. A couple of big shows a year at larger venues does pay well, but not enough to live off of."

"I dig, I just want to play. What little I have played in the time I've been here, nearly a year, hasn't inspired me. Musically I like to mix it up, stretch the boundaries, so to speak. I guess I'm more particular about who I play with than the bread, no pun intended."

Luke smiled, "Let me tell you about The Eclectibles." Five minutes later he finished by saying, "By the end of the year every manager and promoter in Liverpool will know who you are. If you're good enough you'll get offers, you can leave us and Sattie's in the rearview."

Now George smiled, "You wanna see my kit?"

He had walked to the pub so Lucas drove over to his flat. It wasn't a residential neighborhood by any definition. Right on the edge of the waterfront in what was probably an office with an attached workshop. It and the area around it was pretty well maintained; all in all, it seemed a good set-up for George.

They entered the flat, hung a right near the back of the dining nook and entered the shop.

It was a great space, clean, well lit, and heated. An older model estate car was parked inside the single garage door next to a wall that was lined with mechanic's tools. In one of the far corners area rugs dominated, on the floor and walls, forming a cave- like softened retreat. This space contained George's drum set. Lucas had never seen anything like it. Massive, like you could toss a couple of drumsticks into its maw and the thing would come alive.

Double bass drums with the requisite snare and hi-hat, and a sweeping, arced set of tom-toms ranging from big floor toms all the way round to stand mounted eight inchers. More cymbals than you could count on one hand along with triangle, cowbell, and two gongs. All the big names were there like Paiste, Gretsch, Zildjian, and Ludwig. All the bells and whistles, literally, arranged in a circular fashion around a simple round stool.

"Christ, George, it looks like a museum display!"

"Albeit a functional one, my friend. Do you play?"

"Not a lick. I'd like to see you play, though. That is, if you can find a way into that maze."

George chuckled. "Check it out."

Five minutes later Luke was sold. "You wanna meet some of the band?"

They loaded a basic seven-piece kit into the Vauxhall and headed south to Mossley Hill. George talked of his love for motorcycles, he was a Harley guy. He'd sold his hog before coming to England; shipping his kit was the limit. Besides, he needed to get accustomed to the weather and all the traffic conditions before venturing out on two wheels. "I think if I ever get to ride on a regular basis here it'll be on a British bike. I can picture myself cruising the Lake district on a classic Vincent."

"Sweet."

"It's probably for the best now that I abstain. Can't do anything that would keep me from working. Baking and drumming, conversely, complement each other. Baking keeps my neck and shoulders toned."

"That makes sense. Never arm wrestle with a baker."

"I think Confucius said that." That cracked them both up.

"So, who's your favorite drummer, or biggest influence?"

"Impossible to answer. I think once you become one of the best at what you do, it's a unique thing. Like in drumming. Ginger Baker, Keith Moon, Buddy Rich, Gene Krupa, John Bonham, the list goes on. Each has their own style, their own sound. Who can say who's the best? It's personal taste. I guess I admire them all, and I hope my sound reflects that while doing my own thing."

"Sounds like a solid philosophy. Drumming for me is the most Zen like of disciplines in a collection of musicians. It's, I don't know, primal? Like the most basic of instruments, but with the most range of freedom and sound."

"Music to my ears, man. Simpatico! Percussion is the art of one object striking another. A simple concept. But what are these objects made of, how fast are they moving, and at what angle? The weight, the area of contact, and in what type of physical setting? It creates aurality, a combination of tone and timbre, different every time out."

Such heady conversation, continuing all the way home. George was introduced to Daniela and the kids. Cy and the Blues were hosting Brighton at Goodison. Colly and the McTimons went to the match along with Neff and the senior Ardavans. Luke went next door to convene with Obs and Robs.

George hung with Jake and Otter while Dani tended to the baby, enjoying the domestic feel of the setting. Jake was not shy checking out the new visitor with the kind smile and long blonde ponytail, showing him around the house, then inviting him into the garden.

Two doors down the junior Ardavans and the Pines were brought up to speed and were psyched over Luke's account of the day so far. Ben went out back to get the grill going and Abbas rearranged the living and dining areas for a listening session. Faith and Robin went to Dani for some contributions towards a shared supper.

They ate outside, around the firepit, the weather chilly, the conversation warm and lively. George was proving to be a man for all seasons, revealing his past employment as a barber.

"It's all about the hands," he explained. "Actually, it starts with the brain, of course. Sending its message through the neck, shoulders, arms, and into the hands to do its bidding. Cutting hair, baking bread, fixing a bike, and playing drums. Each set of movements its own discipline, feeding the next."

"All day I've been hearing this, it's like talking to the Buddha," Luke teased.

"Sorry, man, I do go on sometimes. You guys've got me all spiked up, the karma here is wonderful!"

"Perhaps we should channel it," Abbas suggested. "Summon the Buddha, the Lama, and the Djinn. Let them guide us, let the energy flow through our instruments."

"Meaning?"

"Let's jam!"

Everyone helped clean up and bring stuff in. The fire pit was doused, the fireplace lit. Faith stayed downstairs with the dogs and kids; the rest went to the attic for an extra dose of karma.

Penny and Bashir came over with their crew. George became enchanted all over again.

Abbas, Robin, and George got into it. Tentative at first, following each other's lead, until all three were locked in on the same groove. After a while they could play without stopping, one teasing a new direction until the other two fell in, a segue to a different sound altogether. From the pastoral to the anthemic, the moods shifted, Faith and Dani lending voice when a familiar melody arose.

It was George's touch that impressed Obs and Robs. Never too heavy-handed, dynamic when needed, he had a feel for when to accompany, and when to stand out.

Time passed quickly, lost in the 'aurality,' as George would say.

The other group came back after the football match, all calling it a night except for Colly, in search of her roomies while waiting for Cy and Shea.

"Here you all are. Wow, it's a party!" She was handed a glass of wine while giving the verdict on the game, suddenly falling silent as she stared at the dude behind the kit. He, too, was mute, agape at her presence.

"George?"

"Colleen?"

"George Pearson?"

"Colleen Baumann?"

They both started laughing. Then hugging and laughing.

"This day has gone from the sublime to the surreal!" he exclaimed.

"George is a close friend of my brother-in-law," she explained. "We've met a handful of times. What brings you to Liverpool, George?"

"I live here. What's your excuse?"

"I live here. My last name is Barcant now."

"Congrats! Wait, as in Cyril Barcant?"

"That's my hubby."

"Damn, girl, a wag you are, as they say."

"So, you've a job here, all legal?"

"Yes, ma'am. A barber, a drummer, and a cake maker."

"Too bad the Beatles broke up, they'd write a song about you," interjected Robin.

"George is our new drummer," Abbas reported.

"Really?" he asked.

"Why not? A better first impression you could not have made."

George put a bear hug on him. "Thanks, man. This is a wonderful thing."

"You know, you resemble Cyril a bit," Ben pointed out. "Geez, with your upper body, and his lower body? Powerful! By the way, Sean Doyle was my roommate for two years down in St. Pete."

"What? At Farragut?" he asked. Ben just nodded. "Whoa, a truly synchronistic consciousness, I better sit down."

They were all up late that night. Cy and Shea got home; the kids were put to bed. A moonlight walk with Otter and Barky around the lake, a midnight toke under the yew.

George crashed on the couch, he and Barky watching the fire die down. Sleep did not come easy for the guy; he'd experienced a Greenbank encounter, and was still feeling the effects.

CHAPTER 41
MONDAY, 1 OCTOBER

*The sight of a touch,
or the scent of a sound,
Or the strength of an oak
with roots deep in the ground*

*Missives from Merseyside
Calderstones Park*

It must've been one of the best days of my life, that day in November of '71. I began my career as a gardener for the City of Liverpool and was assigned to Calderstones Park.

My name is Jon Warren, from Wavertree. Eight years later I'm still at it, and quite happy about it. Sixteen years old I was then, fresh-faced and newly graduated from secondary school, an apprentice position secured in one of the city's jewels.

In the beginning there were a couple dozen of us minding the park, each with their own little patch to tend. Times are harder now; we're forced to team up a bit. Better tools and equipment helps, and it's a great crew we have. It's such a good environment to work in as well, being outdoors in beautiful surroundings. The weather can be dodgy, of course, but for me much better than being anchored to an office.

Calderstones is special; the stones themselves, obviously, are very important relics of pagan times. Both the old English Garden and the Japanese Garden are spectacular, and the Allerton Oak is ancient, reputed to be a thousand years old.

We love the public to come out for a visit and comment on the park. Look me up, we'll have a chat!

Ben had interviewed Jon under the Allerton Oak last month. He felt like he'd made a friend. He was a few years older than his subject, but Jon was not shy, speaking clearly and confidently about his work and general station in life. His countenance, a ruddy exterior and an ever-present smile, would remain etched in Ben's memory.

He took some pictures that day but decided to visit the archives for his choice for the book. The flora in the Japanese Garden was unique and varied. The height of autumn's foliage color change was prime time for a photograph.

He reviewed the shot one last time. This one might be worthy of the book's cover, he thought.

Central was the pond, rocks and boulders in and around it. Several of the evergreens there were sculpted into topiaries, some left natural. Mixed grasses, ferns, and various water plants at pond's edge were adorned with the reds, yellows, and oranges of fallen leaves from the myriad of trees framing the scene. Native and non-native species thrived here, creating a palette to stir the senses.

Yes, this one should do quite nicely!

CHAPTER 42
FRIDAY, 5 OCTOBER

Found my coat and grabbed my hat
Made the bus in seconds flat
Found my way upstairs and had a smoke
And somebody spoke and I went into a dream

Time seemed to accelerate at the beginning of fall. The equinox signaled not only the change of season but also a sort of reset in the mindset of those whose turning of a calendar page was a cause for concern. Not really a reason for worry, just a reminder to heed the call to start another school term, go again on the football pitch, or just rededicate oneself to the challenges of a chosen profession.

Kevin McTimons was immune to the season's call at the moment; the man's head was still filled with tropical breezes. He was at work, preparing to open his chip shop up in Wavertree. Calypso music spilled out of the open door onto High Street, puzzling onlookers going about their day. Kevin was inside, humming along in his Panama shirt. He did have on a proper pair of shoes. His employees had been bemused at

Kevin's demeanor the past week, thinking he should take holidays on a regular basis. If asked he would surely agree.

Dani would sign on for a vacation right now, she was leaning over a microscope looking at a stool sample. Apparently, there was a war waging in the digestive tract of Mrs. Cobb's Pembroke Welsh corgi.

Faith and Colleen would have traded places with Dani, and gladly. They were getting a thorough description of the conflict within Audrey Fulton's large intestine, no details omitted. April decided to go get something from the stockroom.

The situation was a little more 'settled' back home at Greenbank. Over a quarter of its residents were off to school, leaving the three youngest children to look after Cheryl, Aleah, and Neff, supervised by Otter and Isaac.

Bashir and his kids were at Greenbank Primary, and Lucas was at Quarry Bank with Cyrus and Seamus, all playing their parts in the pursuit of academia. Cy was adjusting well to secondary school life, his hunger to learn stronger than his trepidation of oncoming adolescence.

Lucas had changed the way he taught language during his tenure, slowly employing a new approach that, when first noticed by his peers, drew a lot of skepticism. Time had shown a method to his madness though, reflected in his students' marks and improved linguistic abilities.

At the beginning of the term, he would hand out a number of lists containing what to learn if you really wanted to be multi-lingual. Verb conjugations, tenses, sentence structure, and usage, to name a few. In the classroom, Luke's goal was to get his charges motivated to take these lists on as homework, on their own. To do so he told them stories, and showed examples in everyday life. He spoke to them in French, Spanish, Farsi, and German. He even spoke English in a southern drawl, or a western twang, anything to get them desperate to learn language.

On occasion he would bring Cyril, Abbas, or Dani in for a trip to distant lands, stoking the kids' imaginations. Last week he brought in his ace in the hole, Caspar. At seven years old Caspar was bi-lingual in English and Farsi. Luke could see it in their eyes, the possibilities.

Seamus had attended Luke's French class this morning, plus geography and science, but was now free from scholarly teachings in order to attend Cyril's class on the importance of anticipation in the pursuit of winning second balls on a football pitch. It was private instruction; they were sitting together on the Everton team coach on the way down to the Midlands to play at Coventry.

Ben was being tutored as well. Maybe tutored wasn't the correct term; lined out would be more accurate. He was in John's office, who was laying out a smorgasbord of news items confronting the Echo's staff at present.

"It's all hands to the pump today, Ben. I want the weekend editions to grab everyone's attention. The news wires are smoking!"

He was right; dispatches were coming in hot and heavy. The U.S. was about to give Panama its canal back. The Yorkshire Ripper had claimed 20-year-old Barbara Leach as his 12th victim. Mother Teresa was to be awarded the Nobel Peace Prize. The first gay rights march in Washington was cueing up, and the IRA had penetrated the Royal family. The Queen's cousin, Lord Mountbatten, his teenage grandson, and a young deckhand had been murdered aboard Mountbatten's private fishing boat while pulling lobster pots.

"And to top it off," John continued, "the Woolton picture house wants us to run a story on 'The Sound of Music' in advance of their screening of it on the film's 15th anniversary."

"That's not a big deal, 15 years."

"Exactly my point!"

"I have an idea," offered Ben.

"Please!"

"I'll write it, and tell them 'The Sound of Music' is the 'Swiss Family Robinson' of wartime musicals."

You could hear the man laugh all the way down the hall.

Just another day in the life.

CHAPTER 43
TUESDAY, 9 OCTOBER

When I was a child I caught a fleeting glimpse
Out of the corner of my eye

Cyrus was getting the hang of this secondary school thing, now embracing the exact aspects of a further education that, at first, made him feel queasy. It's not that the source of his fears didn't exist. There were bullies, and girls, and teachers whose countenances were impenetrable. So what, he'd survived the same in primary school.

Walking home after his last class on a cold, windy day, his thoughts were on something adults often say to children who, in their view, weren't behaving properly. "Act your age!" they'd say, apparently forgetting that they too were once children. How am I supposed to act my age when I've never been this age before? Wait till I spring that one on them.

Rose and Caspar were also walking home from school, from the opposite direction. They were bundled against the chill, and in deep conversation. Well, Caspar was listening to Rosie talk, as usual. The subject, something she heard the grownups talking about, something she was determined to figure out.

Caspar wasn't as nosy as Rosie, especially when it came to what all the adults were on about. He had no authority in such matters.

Apparently, their father and uncles were going to do something together, possibly something important. He'd be told about it in due time, if at all. It was like that real boss karate guy on the telly said, "Will worry change the future, Grasshopper?"

Rose, conversely, not only wanted to be kept abreast of such discussions, she wanted to be consulted. The girl was curious, and precocious.

Like now, just as we're almost home, she sees a dog in the park, running around on its own. We're supposed to come straight home after school.

Cyrus came to Greenbank Lane; he could see the row houses on the right. Crossing Streatham, he headed for home but was alerted to some noise in the park, someone shouting. It was Rosie. She and Caspar were being accosted by two older boys by the lake. He started to yell when suddenly one of the boys pushed Caspar into the water. He screamed at the front of the house instead, dropping his book bag and sprinting towards the lake.

Before he got there he could see Rosie help Caspar to the shore. Caspar was soaked and sobbing. Rosie was crying too, now trying to get her book bag back, along with Caspar's.

Cy then realized you don't have to go to school to get bullied, it can happen in your own backyard. Something inside of him turned and hardened.

The boys, probably a couple of years older and bigger than he, looked up from rifling through their haul, turning to face him. Cy slowed and made to help his friends. Suddenly he increased his pace and veered to his left; it was three strides and all the momentum he could summon behind his fist exploding into the biggest one's nose and mouth.

It was an epiphany! Feeling the rush he launched into the second guy, locked together, and going to ground, knees and elbows flying.

"Run!" He screamed at Rose as the other guy regained his feet and came for his revenge.

He was getting beaten badly now. The two bigger boys were merciless. He thought of Caspar, the look on his face coming out of the lake and decided Caspar had it worse. One day his pain would go away. Caspar would feel the humiliation for much longer. That's what bullying did to you.

It was decided that Cyrus would get dragged into the water, maybe even held under for a bit, teach the whelp good and proper.

Suddenly a sound announced itself, guttural and with intent. Otter, leaping into the air, all 115 pounds directed into a full body slam. He didn't bite the kid, but the noises he was making made both boys mewl in fear. They both dove into the lake, Otter in pursuit.

"He's an Otterhound, you idiots!" Cy let the three splash about for a bit before calling the dog back in. The two boys got out of the water 30 yards down the bank and took off.

He turned to see his mum under the yew, Poppy in her arms, Gabe and Jake sheepishly clinging to her housecoat. Rosie and Caspar helped him across the street and into the house.

A split lip, bruised ribs, probably a black eye in the morning.

"I think he knows who it was," Cheryl said later that evening after supper. "Why won't he tell us?"

"Part of the code," Kevin explained. "He'll get more respect not telling, especially being new at Quarry Bank."

"So, their reputation is more important than getting beaten?"

"Absolutely. Don't worry dear, he'll tell Shea. And I promise ya, Shea will sort it."

Chapter 44
Thursday, 18 October

She walked up to me so gracefully
and took my crown of thorns
"Come in," she said, "I'll give you
shelter from the storm"

Catherine Barcant was turning the tables on her brother and his partner in prankdom.

On a previous visit to Merseyside, Cyril and Lucas had sprung her and Dani's sister, Astrid, on the entire Greenbank collective on Dani's birthday. A massive surprise that included, and concluded, with a marriage proposal. Well now, the worm has turned, as they say. The flip side of the saga would see the response. A kind of karmic realignment.

Kevin collected her and Millie from the train station midday, settling at Greenbank and getting acquainted, and reacquainted with Cheryl, Neff, Aleah, and the young children. Millie was already proving to be a big hit with the gang.

Later in the afternoon Kevin drove Catty up to Bellefield. She and Cyril needed to have a chat, Shea could ride home with his dad.

The reunion was priceless. Catherine stood alone, outside of the training ground's main building. She wasn't immediately recognizable, bundled against the chill in a hat and scarf, but she was noticeable, all the lads sneaking a peek on the way to the car park. Cyril and Seamus came out together, hardly giving her a second glance.

"You boys look useful, can I catch a ride?" Her lilt gave her away.

"Cat!" They hugged it up. Cyril was joyous.

"Seamus! Lawd sakes, what have dey been feeding you?" He got a hug and a kiss.

"Hi Catherine. It's so good to see you, and I shall never forget this day. Well done!"

"Come on son, let's let these two catch up."

The girls had taken the McTimons up on their offer to stay with them, Cheryl was delighted. Kevin, Seamus, and Cyrus were beyond delighted.

Millie had traveled extensively, and was enamored with all the world had to offer. She was also frustrated that her career as a stewardess afforded her with only the rare opportunity to actually become familiar with the places she visited. Her travel experience was limited to airplanes, airports, shuttles, and hotels. All the stuff you'd want to get out of the way so you could actually enjoy your time away from home.

This trip was so wonderfully different. She was waited on the whole way over, she was picked up at the train station, and now she was staying at a friend's home, with her lover and her brother, and a bunch of folks who were treating her like family.

A happy hour was planned in Neff's garden before dinner. The festivities had gotten underway before the quartet had returned from Bellefield.

It was cold but dry, and mostly calm. Faith and Penny supplied extra clothing for Millie: coat, hat, scarf, and the like. She was tall, nearly the limit for her line of work, she had said. Dani and Colly were Catty-sized, so they would outfit her against the chill.

The firepit was cranking, a table was loaded with munchies, and a stereo was cranking out *Rubber Soul*. The gang was filtering in, each one getting their own private dose of Millie, her Caribbean accent like a song.

Kevin, Catty, and Shea got home and went to get ready to join the rest. Cyril went straight into the garden.

"Hey all!"

"Cyril!"

He knew this poor girl was on a knife's edge right now; so much of what was so important to her would be revealed in the next moments.

Millie was looking cool and calm. It's part of what she did for a living. Inside she was a mess, Cyril had just walked in. Where was Catherine? Oh God, here he comes.

Cy looked non-committal as he walked towards her, pausing to pet Barky and tousle Caspar's hair.

"Millicent." He held her hand in both of his, then kissed it. "You have made my sister very happy. I have wondered for some time now if this kind of happiness was possible for her." Then he smiled. It was the kind of smile that made you feel welcome, loved, and safe. "I'm so happy to meet you." With that he hugged her, and she melted.

"Come na, child," brushing a tear off her cheek, "Now we fete for so!" He turned to the rest of the group, kind of mousey they were, not wanting to interrupt or sure about the conversation.

"Why de hesitation? I am a sensitive, new-age, renaissance type of fellow, don't ya know?"

Much frivolity ensued.

CHAPTER 45
WEDNESDAY, 24 OCTOBER

And every one of them words rang true
And glowed like burnin' coal

Lucas got his comeuppance just a little later that same evening. The last to turn up, he had George Pearson in tow. Together they'd taken some of George's drums up to the Dovey for a weekend workout.

Enthused at the soiree going down, they'd strolled into Neff's garden waving and nodding, grabbing a beer, all while getting the sniff-down from security.

"Otter, get off me, man!"

"Luke, this one's got his nose right between the twins!"

"Barky!"

Luke looked around for his kin and to see where he might begin to mingle. Whoa! Who is that?

A stunning blonde, an old school Carnaby Street vibe going on, combination Bond girl and Twiggy.

She was talking to the elder Ardavans, Hassan and Aleah looking captivated, on an intellectual level, far different than the appeal he was feeling at the moment.

Just then, another vision swept past. She came from behind him, through the gate, only her long sun blessed hair any clue as to her identity.

And she glided straight over to the blonde, who turned towards her and smiled, locking arms, and resuming the conversation.

Over by the firepit, Dani, Penny, and Cheryl were preaching the gospel of Luke to Faith, Robin, and Colleen, the lot of them much amused.

"I can't believe it!"

"He's dumbstruck!"

"Take notice, ladies," Dani advised, "You're not likely to see that look ever again."

Penny just laughed.

Cat knew it was Lucas, and purposely strode past, keeping her back to him. After a minute or so she relented and turned to flash him a smile.

Luke had no words for the last three or four minutes, only grateful that Cat ended her charade and ran to embrace him, giving him the chance to bury his red face into the nape of her neck.

"You are priceless," he said, kissing her forehead.

The Ardavans were being waylaid by Rose and Jacob, Millie taking the opportunity to slip away and get introduced to Lucas.

"Well played, m'lady," he complimented, exchanging pleasantries. "It's a pleasure."

Cat took Millie's hand and looked at Lucas, her eyes searching for recognition, judgement, acceptance? She wasn't exactly sure.

"Yeah, you had me bewildered, I must admit. One thing's certain though, you both look very happy together. And you make for a striking couple."

He got a double hug for that.

Happy hour turned into a couple of hours, everyone making merry. Some meat was put on the grill, some veggies steamed, and a salad tossed.

Bedtime came at a reasonable hour; it was a school night and the Trinis needed to shed their jet lag.

They spent Friday around the house and the neighborhood, spending the day with the homebodies.

Saturday was special; another edition of the Merseyside Derby, this one at Anfield. Neff took Cat and Millie, along with George, a new experience for the yank. Pints at the Sandon with Neff and his cronies, followed by all that was Anfield thrilled the three initiates. The match ended in a two all draw, Shea getting on for the last twenty minutes. The lad gave a good account of himself, his first experience in the cauldron of derby football.

There was a Sunday roast at the Dovey, followed by an hour plus of Eclectibles music. This was the first time George and Mike Pinder had jammed together. Mike was impressed, George was starstruck.

It was a field trip for the youngsters on Monday. Millie was raised Catholic and had heard about the Metropolitan Cathedral, up on Hope Street on the edge of the university campus. The building's design was somewhat controversial, the locals dubbing it 'Paddy's Wigwam,' after its exterior's shape and appearance. The inside was magnificent, however. No one would argue that. Awe inspiring.

All four sets of parents at Greenbank had their own religious beliefs and leanings, but all were pretty much in agreement when it came to the children. They wanted them to be exposed to all faiths, and their particular teachings and practices; to learn that God is referred to by many names and worshipped in many different ways. One day they can choose how they want to express their own spirituality.

Cye flew in from Florida yesterday. It was a planned trip, but he didn't know that Cyril's sister and friend were in town. Aleah went to pick him up, taking Cat and Millie along for a little surprise. It very definitely worked.

"Is there no end to the amount of charming, lovely ladies in this city?" The four had lunch in the City Centre, Cye, Cat, and Millie getting acquainted before going home to the zoo.

Well, all good things must pass. Didn't one of the Beatles say that? Regardless, this morning marked the end of a wonderful week for everyone involved. Cyril and Seamus dropped the pair off at Lime Street Station; they had training to go to, the girls a train to catch.

Cyril shared a tender moment with Catherine, their relationship stronger than ever.

For Shea? Just showing up can prove serendipitcus, he got on the receiving end of a double dose of island love.

CHAPTER 46
FRIDAY, 26 OCTOBER

The thirst that from the soul doth rise
Doth ask a drink divine;
But might I of Jove's nectar sup,
I would not change for thine

Missives from Merseyside
The Baltic Fleet

Me names Bertie. Well, to be all proper like, Roberta Ferguson, you would say. No one would know who you were on about though, it's always been Bertie.

I'm the one to tell ya about the Baltic, ave been there longer than the proprietor. Came with the rats, as they say on the docks.

It's where all the business came from, in the old days. Just a lass I was then. From all over they came, wools, bogs from Norway, the Paddys, even ships from the Americas.

Scousers as well. They worked the docks. A hard lot, but mostly on the up, all with a fancy for a pint and a laugh.

The docks went dark for a good long while. And now the Iron Lady's on Downing Street and likely to scupper the whole town, she is.

Our customers are a real mixed bag. Auld pensioners, constantly on a bifter. Scally meffs, ketwig straight up in the air. Soft lads, already bevvy, fancy kecks and webs.

"There's council juice in the tap!" this one daft geezer tells me, so ees only drinking ale.

It's a good thing we have James, a sound lad he is. Looks after the place proper, the Baltic is the place for ale and a chippy.

James can sort the customers, I can tell ya. The scurrilous are told to sod off, the devoed walk in and are marched right back out. The high and mighty, with their jarg trainers, geggin in about their bin color when I'm all chocka, James sorts it.

He's a soft side, as well, our James, giving scran to the skint at Crimbo, or just fixing me a cuppa, sitting down for a chat when me eads all done in. James never swerves it.

As for me, well, it's simple really. The Baltic Fleet is my story, one I'll not shy away from. Pop in sometime, I'll pull ye a pint, listen to yer tales, and serve you up a bowl of the best scouse on Merseyside. Cheers!

Cyril was right, Bertie's a peach! Ben was glad he taped the interview. Now he was thinking if this book gets distributed beyond Liverpool, he might want to include a Scouse to English appendix.

The pub was nearly triangular in shape, constructed to fit its allotted space at the confluence of Wapping, Hurst, and Cornhill. Choosing the angle to compose a photograph was easy, due north of the pub, the more rounded end front and center, the sign in gold block letters on a black background. The shot was taken on a blustery day, the indirect lighting highlighting the white framed windows in their gray walls.

Ben was treated that day. He remembered James had a pint for him, Bertie a bowl of scouse. She was right, it was the best.

CHAPTER 47
THURSDAY, 1 NOVEMBER

Bird of Paradise — Fly
In white sky
Blues for Allah
In'sh' Allah
Let's see with our heart these things our eyes have seen

The Ardavan brothers had always felt that this time would come, a time when tradition and spirituality would combine to issue the call to make the most pious of commitments to Islam. Together they were traveling to Mecca, to make the Hajj.

Muslims lived by a set of tenets, the five pillars of Islam. The first, Shahadah, was simply a declaration of faith, a sincerity in devotion. The next three, Salah, Zakah, and Sawm, were guides for prayer, charity, and fasting. The fifth was the Hajj.

The Hajj was expected of all males, as long as they were physically able and could afford to do so, at least once in their lifetime.

Mecca is the destination, the holiest of cities, birthplace of Muhammad, the prophet. According to the Quran, the Hajj traces back even further, to the time of Abraham.

Held every year, the Hajj takes place during the last month of the Islamic calendar, based on the lunar year. This year that meant the 30th of October through the 3rd of November. The boys had left last Sunday and would return next Monday.

Cye had a nice visit with the gang, he'd spent five days on Merseyside before going to Saudi Arabia. He also brought some news, huddling with Dani before making it public. He and Astrid had become lovers.

"He was nervous," Dani said, sitting with Luke and Robin in Penny's house after dinner. "Like he was asking my dad for her hand in marriage."

"Adorable!" said Penny.

"That shy, quiet middle sibling thing, I guess," Luke surmised. "A big step for him, I'm sure."

"I think he's dreamy," Robin cooed, "All smoldery and mysterious."

"He's an egghead, her too." Penny declared. "A match made in heaven."

"I'm gonna have to give Astrid a call. I wonder if she has told my folks."

"And how about you two, all set?" Penny asked, looking at Luke and Robin.

"Yeah, it's sorted. I'll load the Victor up in the morning and walk to school. Robin will pick me up and we should be there before dark."

Two days ago, the Moody Blues manager, Tony Secunda, had tracked Luke down in a panic. The Moody's had a concert booked in London on Sunday, a one off, and needed a violinist when the one they had lined up had taken ill.

Robin was dying for a chance to gain the type of exposure an event like this would bring, but wouldn't leave Gabriel when Abbas was away. After much discussion and assurances, she relented, and was now getting pretty excited about the idea.

"Time to cut the cord, luv," Penny had gently advised. "You've got your in-laws and an entire rowhouse of willing protectors. Go and show yourself off!"

So, Luke and Tony cut a deal, the manager the latest to succumb to the charms and wiles of the 'Fixer.' The pair would arrive in London tomorrow evening and be back in Liverpool by noon Monday. Abbas and his brothers would return late that night.

The three were halfway through the required duties and rites needed to fulfill their commitment to the Hajj; each step since their arrival was strictly orchestrated.

Mecca lies in a desert valley near Jeddah, close to the Red Sea. It is a city open only to Muslims, accessible by four entrances, the Mawaqeets. Pilgrims cleanse themselves here, begin their period of abstinence, and change clothing in order to attain Ihram, a state of holiness.

Two white, seamless cloths are donned, one a wrap extending from the waist to below the knee. The other is draped over the left shoulder and tied on the right side.

Afterwards, at the Al-Masjid Al-Haram, the mosque itself, the Tawaf is observed by walking counter-clockwise seven times around the Kaaba, a square, almost cube-like building in which the Black Stone, a relic reputed to date back to Adam and Eve, is set in its eastern edge. Then, after prayers, Sa'ay is performed by running, or walking, seven times between the hills of Safa and Marwah. Sa'ay is followed by a haircut, which completes the Umrah, readying a person to perform the rites of the Hajj itself.

The first day is spent traveling to Mina, where afternoon, evening, and night prayers are offered, a day of deep reflection.

The second day, Arafah, sees the pilgrims arrive on the plains of Arafat for an afternoon vigil, to repent and atone for past sins, and listen to sermons from Islamic scholars. After sunset they spend the night on open ground at Muzdalifah, an area between Arafat and Mina. Here they are under the stars, the solemnity of the occasion fueling their prayers and contemplation.

The Ardavans had just completed the third day of the Hajj. After morning prayers, they had gone back to Mina for the Ramy Al-Jamarat, the symbolic stoning of the devil. Three pillars stood there, each pilgrim throwing seven stones at the largest, the Jamrat Al-Aqabah.

To celebrate the story of Abraham and his son Ishmael, animals were sacrificed after the stoning of the devil. In modern times, due to the sheer numbers of people, vouchers were purchased to allow abattoirs to slaughter and process the meat and distribute it charitably.

Another haircut, this time a proper buzz cut, ended the day. Preparing for bed, Abbas warned the other two, "This will not go unnoticed at home."

Chapter 48
Monday, 5 November

Leave the wise to write
for they write worldly rhymes
And he who wants to fight
begins the end of time

The first Monday of November was one of note, a fluid, ever enlightening variety of events, resulting in a roller coaster of emotions. Ben was the first to get his beginning of the week bubble burst, soon after arriving at work. Just wait till the final edition of the Echo hit the streets.

Next was the former pilgrims, preparing to head for the airport and a flight home. News like this was of greater interest in this part of the world.

One by one, the remaining members of the clan, at least the adults, caught wind of events elsewhere during their normal routines, another 'oh, did you hear,' kinda moment.

The last to be enlightened was Luke and Robin. They'd been in a different world the past 72 hours, and the news had nearly quite literally stopped them in their tracks.

Up until now everything was unfolding according to plan. There was no describing the emotions Bashir, Cye, and Abbas felt upon fulfilling the rites of the Hajj, outwardly manifested in the calm, serene countenance they displayed.

The last two days of the pilgrimage entailed more stoning of the devil, along with much prayer and reflection. The brothers also performed the Tawaf again. This time the crowds had thinned; they were able to touch the sacred Black Stone.

They could have started their journey home yesterday but were glad they stayed to observe the first day of the Eid Al-Adha, the Feast of the Sacrifice. The holiday further celebrates the story of Abraham's willingness to sacrifice his son, Ishmael.

According to legend, Allah was satisfied with Abraham's loyalty and sent the angel Gabriel with a lamb to slaughter in Ishmael's stead. The lamb is divided between family, friends, and the poor.

Nearly 800,000 of the faithful had made the Hajj this year, Muslims from all over the world regardless of race, color, or culture. Malcolm X had been here in the '60s. He left admitting to a fundamental change in his thinking with regard to race relations. Such was the spirit and feeling of brotherhood he'd experienced while in Mecca.

The Ardavans felt it as well. After nearly a week of cleansing, prayer, duty, and piety, it was a joy just to be in the company of and converse with their fellow pilgrims.

Lucas had been thinking of his Persian pals for most of the week. He knew the significance of what they'd experienced, and the extent of the commitment they'd made. Then came the call from Tony Secunda, refocusing and commanding his attention.

His love for Robin had grown in the last four days. What a treat it was seeing the change in her emotions play out, and to see her respond to the situation.

She was thrilled at the offer, a night on the big stage, followed by disappointment when she thought she couldn't go. Then, appreciation for the gang's support and encouragement.

She had sat in the back on the way down, an open case, set lists, and sheet music scattered about as she coaxed the Moody's tunes from her instrument. It beat hell out of the radio.

They had a room booked at a hotel within walking distance of Wembley Arena, where the concert was to be held. Formerly the Empire Pool, Wembley was an indoor arena next to the national team outdoor stadium. They showered, had dinner in the hotel restaurant, then took a long walk to work out the travel stiffness. This area northwest of the center of London was nice, mostly upscale. Gentrified, you might say.

Saturday was a busy day for Robin. There were rehearsals at the venue, tomorrow's set list was decided, and she met the band.

The lads were friendly and gracious, asking after Abbas and reliving his tour with them five years ago. Mike Pinder, a part-time Eclectible, had been replaced with Swiss keyboardist Patrick Moraz.

Robin had an extra session with the other two supplemental musicians, Mary Sumner and Beth Paige, a violist and a cellist, respectively. Luke treated the three to dinner that night, fascinated to listen in on their shop talk.

They slept in on Sunday, then went sightseeing down by the Thames, places like Westminster and Buckingham and Hyde Park.

The gig was fantastic! Luke sat side stage and was immersed; this was a polished, fine-tuned outfit. They had a big catalog to choose from, and obliged with plenty of hits and a few deep tracks.

Beth, Robin, and Mary were great, shaking off some early jitters with a lively performance punctuated with quality musicianship. The Moody's were appreciative, giving them their due with the audience, and making way for them to solo.

Luke and Robin's appearance at the after party was brief.

"Don't lose my number," Robin said on their way out.

"Tell your agent to take it easier on me next time," was Tony's retort.

They were off at first light this morning, happily talking over their weekend and looking forward to getting home. The trip was non-eventful, and they were making good time. Robin turned on the radio just an hour from Liverpool. A complete shock.

The U.S. Embassy in Tehran had been taken over by Iranian militants, seizing nearly a hundred personnel, now hostages.

Luke was incensed, although he wasn't totally surprised. Jimmy Carter was a good guy, but his continued support of the Shah was puzzling. The revolution had given the clerics and hard-liners control of the country; the failure to bring the Shah to 'justice' left a bad taste in their mouths. Ten days ago is when yesterday's storming of the embassy actually took root. Carter had admitted the Shah into the United States in order to undergo cancer treatment at New York's Cornell Medical Center. Again, Washington's inability to understand Islam and its ways had bit them in the ass. Still, Luke was irate. The staff at the embassy was undeserving of being targeted. These people knew Iran, and were there to strengthen relations.

Events elsewhere did not dampen the reunion at Greenbank. Cheryl and Aleah unleashed the hounds and the hellions on the pair before they could get in the door.

Throughout the afternoon the gang filtered in, students and workers coming home, bathing, eating, spending time with the rest.

Ben worked late. Mondays were busy as a rule, today was on steroids.

Lucas, Penny, and Robin went to Lime Street Station just before nine. The girls put some lovin' on their guys, and Luke greeted each formally, in Farsi, addressing them using the honorific Hajji before their name.

The kids were in bed when they arrived home. Ben had some details from Tehran, the adults talked till midnight.

CHAPTER 49
SUNDAY, 11 NOVEMBER

I can hear your words
When you speak of what you are and have seen
I can see your hand
Reaching out through a shining daydream
Where the days and nights are not the same
Captured happy in a picture frame

She didn't know why such a fuss was being made, even more so than usual. She would not understand why, even if told. Nothing these people said made sense, and they didn't get her either. No matter, everyone seemed happy around her, today especially.

Poppy Anne Carter had just completed her first trip around the sun.

"Happy Birthday, sweetie!" Faith said, balancing Poppy on her knee, the infant leaning forward, both arms wrapped around Faith's basketball sized belly. "Soon you won't be the youngest amongst us."

"You're ready, aren't you Faith?" asked Cyril.

"More than ready, Cy. I can't say I'm that uncomfortable, for the most part. Anxious mostly, I suppose."

"You are pretty big, if I may," Abbas dared.

"Immense is more like it. They'll be assigning me my own post code soon!"

Most of the gang was in the Pine-Ardavan house, the twenty somethings anyway, kids and dogs scattered about. Plans for the day included some exercise before lunch and late afternoon band practice at the Dovey.

Things were pretty much back to normal at Greenbank after an eventful past few weeks. All was not right in the world; however, Ben had gathered some updates on Iran during the week. He and Luke were trying to predict the future.

Islamic rule was well established now; holy wrath was still raining down on those deemed responsible for the pre-revolution state of the nation. The number of executions exceeded five hundred. There were still names on the list.

Some of the hostages taken at the embassy were freed, a list of the fifty-two remaining had been released. Among them were the two 'company' men that tried to recruit Luke, Tom Ahern and William Daugherty. Also on the list was one Colonel Leland 'Lee' Holland. Luke was sad and mad.

"Something should have been done by now! What the fuck!"

"They probably have the hostages spread out," Ben offered. "So a rescue isn't possible."

"Zealots aren't easy to negotiate with either," added Cy. "If they're talking at all."

"What about some kind of third party getting involved? Some nation, or organization making a plea?"

"It would have to be from Muslims," Abbas said. "Religion is what's been driving this situation from the beginning. The Ayatollah needs to be reminded of what the Quran teaches."

"Well said Abbas," Colleen remarked.

"The Ayatollah has power now. Power corrupts," Robin said.

"I feel helpless just sitting here while innocent people suffer, if they're not being executed," Luke agonized.

"Nothing we can do, noble mon."

"I guess you're right," Ben said. "Seems like we could do something though."

"How about . . ." Luke started.

"Hey!" It was Dani, now standing. "You two listen to me! I neutered both your dogs; don't think I won't do the same to the both of you!"

"Let's change the subject," Abbas suggested.

"Let's talk about Faith's belly," Cyril ventured. Faith gave a half chuckle, not amused.

"Snip! Snip!" Dani warned.

"Maybe we should go outside for recess," Robin advised.

Four hours later the birthday girl and her entourage were making their way up Penny Lane when a vehicle slowed beside them, the driver rolling down his window.

"You can't assemble this many people and have a parade without a permit!" It was Paul Pilnik.

"Ya bunch of hippies!" Geoff Higgins was in the passenger seat.

George Pearson and Mike Pinder were already at the pub, setting up. Neither had brought their full rigs but a wide array of equipment was present.

Gillian and Emma were at the taps, along with April and Colin, the new guy. Gilly hired a man this time, for several reasons. He was experienced, and he could provide some help with security. Also, he was less likely to run off with someone affiliated with Greenbank. April was part-time now, only working now and then.

Dani and Colleen had made cupcakes, like about fifty of them, each with a single candle, now on trays at the end of the bar. Anyone could have one, the only stipulation being you had to light the candle and blow it out with Poppy.

When the stage was set, the Eclectibles and their manager, pints in hand, went out the back and onto the green for a puff and a pow wow.

"What's new, gaffer?" Mike asked.

"Well, the date's set, two weeks from today. I've got John and Angus on board. Tickets are printed and go on sale tomorrow, twelve quid a pop." He hesitated, "And yes, I got us the Phil."

George's eyes glazed over, nearly rolling back in his head as he slowly, reverently intoned, "The Royal Liverpool Philharmonic Hall."

The music was spirited and fluid, everyone now eyeing the prize.

Geoff and George had formed a solid partnership on the bottom end, Dani and Faith were in fine voice, and harmonizing well with the back-ups, and the rest were in sync, in combination or solo.

Every session was adding confidence, and quality, and Luke still wasn't done behind the scenes.

Gilly leaned against the bar, a knowing smile on her face, shaking her head. George and April were making eyes at each other.

"Here we go again."

CHAPTER 50
SUNDAY, 18 NOVEMBER

'Cause we gonna lay around the shanty, mama,
And put a good buzz on

It was the rawest day of the season so far. A system had blown in off the Irish Sea over the weekend, leaving Liverpool wet, windy, and very cold. The Greenbank gang were in hibernation.

Bashir and Penny were dealing with it sensibly, in housecoats and thick socks, in the front room next to a blazing fire. Rose and Caspar were sipping hot chocolate and watching the telly, Isaac digging the smells.

Bashir was in his chair, perusing today's Echo. He noticed Penny had sat at the table, putting pen to paper.

"What's that?"

"Nothing really, yet. I'm trying to write a song."

"Oh?"

"Yeah, it's something I've got on with Cyrus. We're going to be lyricists for the Eclectibles. His words, not mine."

"Clever boy. I miss him at school."

"He's adorable. Cheer up, you get Jacob next year."

"I'll need to buck up for that. Lucas, the sequel."

"And our nephew the year after."

"What a pair!"

When the program was over, Caspar started on a puzzle and Rosie got her Crayolas, a peaceful family scene playing out. Bashir returned to his paper, leaving Penelope alone with her thoughts.

She was composing an ode to a couple of cats that lived down on the docks. They weren't feral, but they were orphans, relying on each other to survive the weather, the lack of food, and the sporadic ill nature of mankind. She was determined, somehow, to make it a cheery tune.

Next door, Div and Pari had no such hardships to endure; these cats had it made. They were presently stretched out on an old loveseat cushion by the fire. The warmth, combined with full bellies after kibble and milk, had them sedate and sleepy, one ear on half duty.

The smell of coffee was strong downstairs in Neff's house. He and Hassan were at the table pouring over building specifications instead of song lyrics. Ardavan Concepts and Design was as busy as it wanted to be, with not a farthing spent in the way of advertising or marketing. George Stillwell found the clients and the clients furnished the property. Hassan reimagined the property for its intended future use and Neff made sure everything was kosher with the powers that be. The firm's portfolio was growing, its body of work preserved in files containing drawings, specs, proposals, and two 8 x 10 glossies, before and after, courtesy of Benjamin Pine.

Aleah sat by the front window, gazing out at the frosty scene Mother Nature had served up today. She was deep in thought, feeling a bit at the crossroads. In a good way, mind you, she felt it was time to reestablish a balance in her life that had been absent for some time.

It seemed strange to feel guilty, but that's what it was. She finally figured it out, a nagging tug at her sense of duty.

She'd been rescued, literally, nine months ago, her homeland reduced to a killing ground. It had shaken her to the core, something only time could ameliorate. But she hadn't been placed in a refugee camp, or processed into a compound somewhere strange, waiting for assignment to a country she'd barely even heard of. She'd actually been escorted, safely and comfortably, to a place she knew fairly well, surrounded by friends and family, a new life.

She did need time, to recover and reset herself; that box had been checked. Now it was time to get productive, to give back.

Times were hard, presently. Great Britain was in a financial tailspin. School budgets were meager and stretched, the children the ones to suffer in the end. Aleah was a teacher, an art teacher, and kids needed to learn more than just the ABCs, they needed a well-rounded curriculum to enrich their education.

An old used car, one like the boys had, with plenty of space to haul supplies around in, that was job one. Then a list, public schools, not private, the poorer ones that needed help most. She would go and offer herself, time and materials, wherever they'd have her.

She was glad to have this little talk with herself, already feeling more at ease, more 'in balance.'

One door down Aleah's other son and daughter-in-law were still abed, post -coital, snuggled up together.

"Well, that surely did the trick."

"Well, we'll have to try a few more times just to make sure."

"If you insist."

They were indeed trying to get pregnant again. Gabe was three already. Where did all that time go, and they didn't want too big a gap in their children's ages.

"Tell you what, we'll just keep at it till we get it right."

"With pleasure, m'lady."

Their existing progeny was downstairs hanging with the roomies.

"Baky go bafwoom?"

"He's already gone, Gabe. It's too cold to stay outside."

"Okay."

"How 'bout some juice. Or maybe . . . hot chocolate?"

"Hachacca!"

"Yeah, hachacca!"

Faith was in the kitchen, listening. This house was full of little boys, she thought. Then she wondered, am I about to drop another little rascal into our lives? Boy or girl, she always said she really didn't care, but it would be nice for Poppy to have a girlfriend to run with. Useless to ponder, they'd all know soon enough. Speak of the devil.

"Faith, I've just come up with something brilliant!"

"Oh?"

"Absolutely. You know how it's kind of awkward, when anyone talks about the baby. They hesitate, like they start to say boy, or girl, and realize nobody knows, and they don't want to say it? That's just kinda weird."

"Yes."

"Okay, so we give our baby a name now."

"But you just said nobody knows, boy or girl."

"Exactly! So, we give the baby a name that's neither."

"Like what?"

"Splinter."

"You've gone daft!"

"Think about it. It's a silly name, so it won't be growing on us. Then after the baby's born we can change it."

"Splinter, what's a splinter?"

"A little baby pine."

Her laughter hastened the Ardavans out of bed.

"What's happening?"

It would've awakened the McTimons next door as well, but they were all up and at 'em. Ian was home.

It was a planned trip, his first back to Liverpool since he'd gone to live with Ben's folks.

He arrived at Heathrow yesterday in time to take the tube over by Highbury Stadium in North London, stashing his suitcase and claiming the will call ticket for him to attend the Arsenal-Everton match.

Seeing his brother play for Everton brought tears to his eyes. The kid was becoming a solid professional footballer, putting in a proper shift and showing some cheek in the process. Cyril Barcant, as usual, one of the class players in the whole league, raged in midfield, the Toffees dismissing the Gunners efforts two-nil.

Mick Lyons talked the gaffer into putting Ian on the team bus home, that alone being the thrill of a lifetime. He knew a handful of the lads. The trip flew by, Ian leading the chorus with his flute.

The McTimons had planned to sleep in but were too spiked up. Ian, Shea, and Cyrus went out with Luke and the dogs for the morning business. When they returned their mum was up and busy in the kitchen, their dad banking the fire, anticipating a day at home with all their boys.

Cyril was the last out of bed at the north end of the rowhouse, presently luxuriating in a steamy hot shower, loosening up the joints and muscles that had, once again, served him well on the pitch.

Dani and Colleen were in the kitchen, putting together an easy breakfast so they could loll about. Fruit, porridge, and crusty bread was on the morning's menu.

In the front room Jacob was giving his little sister walking lessons. He stood facing her, holding both hands, walking slowly backwards. This she was good at, giggly with every step. Then he tried it one handed. At first she reached for him, not good for balance, until she got it down after a few steps. Then she was motoring solo, and doing well, staying upright until the excitement of the whole thing got the best of her, and she would topple.

Otter was amused, on his haunches adjacent to the fire, gnawing on a soupbone. The big guy loved the whelps. They grew up so fast. He and Barky, and Isaac, for that matter, knew how it was with human pups. Pretty much worthless at first, only becoming less messy and more interesting after they were weaned. Once they began to get mobile is when the big dogs took notice, the time when it was part of their job to look after them.

There were perks, extra food when they were sloppy, and better lovin' after they got big enough, and learned all the right places to scratch and rub. There was an awkward phase, when they started getting bossy, even though they were incorrect in their decisions and commands.

But, like dogs, the humans got it more or less together by the time they were full grown. This Otter didn't know from experience; he hadn't seen any pup from a human litter grow up all the way. He could see the results, though; the big ones that were properly trained were the alphas.

All the Greenbank gang were aware that the afternoon and evening would force a call to action; a group this large could not remain idle for a 24-hour period.

Ben was requested to shoot a McTimons family portrait. The one he'd taken of the Ardavans when Cye was here was a big hit.

Colly and Penny were going to spend a couple of hours at Erins Pharmacy, furthering Pen's ability to help out more when Faith was on maternity leave.

There was band practice at the Dovey. Ian was going to sit in with the group this session.

Neff, Aleah, and Hassan were having dinner at the Stillwell's; the boys were going to plan for next week.

Some of the other activities slated were more mundane, errands and the like. All in due time, for now everyone was more than content, thank you very much.

CHAPTER 51
SUNDAY, 25 NOVEMBER

There's a band out on the highway,
they're high-steppin' into town
It's a rainbow full of sound

The Eclectibles were never likely to reach their commercial potential, the reasons varied, and indistinct. Certainly, the collective was talented, committed, and got on well. Experience wasn't an issue, and they certainly weren't naive.

It just didn't happen. No one was bummed, or ready to scuttle the project, it just evolved that way. The fact that the band, any band, could even remain active and not be at odds for ten years was no mean accomplishment.

In the end, the band's principals, Obs and Robs, had not wanted to compromise their commitment to family. Life in a successful recording and performing group required constant touring. Typically, it's one spouse on the road months at a time. Abbas and Robin both were Eclectibles; Gabriel would end up being raised by the gang.

The rest of the band understood, and, knowing how personal the dynamic was among all involved, probably sensed it from the start. Most of them had lived that life and were free to return to it, as Aynsley Dunbar had done. Mike had even returned to the Moodys for a while, but now was back. Certainly, Dani and Faith would not abandon their careers to become nomads.

Luke had spent much time pondering such matters and had come to the conclusion that things were just fine as they stood. Every band member had their own side gigs necessary to pay the bills, which left them free to create something together under no pressure whatsoever. It wasn't a job, and the joy they played with, along with their obvious skill, was the reason they were so damn good, and such a thrill to see perform.

Once or twice a year they took to the big stage; tonight was such an occasion. It was Lucas' chance to act the proper manager, a challenge he relished. His duties included booking a venue, getting tickets printed and sold, putting together a stage crew, and taking care of all his contacts imposed upon necessary to accomplish the mission.

In the past five years he'd steered the band into Liverpool's most iconic performance halls, Mountford, the Cavern Club, the Everyman, and the Empire among them.

Tonight it was the Royal Symphony's Philharmonic Hall, the city's acoustic gold standard. It was, by far, the most expensive venue to book, prompting Luke to reset the ticket price at 15 pounds. It was worth it; the Hall's management provided a turnkey package. They would handle ticket sales, provide ushers, security, and assistance for John Price and Angus Rigby, the group's light and sound guys. Luke told the Phil not to bother with marketing the show, just announce when tickets would go on sale, and prepare for the crush.

The hall wasn't easy to book. Only three rock acts, Pink Floyd, Deep Purple, and Elton John, had ever performed there. Luke made a few well-placed calls and paid a couple of timely visits, and it was done, the cost being a couple of reserved loge boxes.

With all the main details looked after, he turned to the smaller tasks, wanting to make sure this event was not only memorable, but completely unforgettable. He drafted Aleah to adorn the stage, who in turn enlisted Gillian and Phillippa Carter as her assistants. Apparently the three had shared their love of the arts during a conversation at the garden party, back in August.

He also, after a recent conversation with George, went to a handful of music stores and bought an array of noisemakers for the band. Tambourine, maracas, shakers, castanets, some chimes, a djembe, and, of course, a cowbell. Stands to hang them on would sit on each side of the stage.

For an encore Luke had 1,000 buttons made, featuring a black background on which Eclectibles was printed in white, each letter in a different script. These he got through the kind ladies at the News From Nowhere bookstore, who always had a big assortment of counterculture buttons in their shop. The first fans through the door would go home with a souvenir other than their ticket stub.

Abbas sat at the dining table, pouring over the evening's set list. He'd come up with the idea of paying homage to the venue by playing a series of mini symphonies, each one featuring a different sub-genre of music. Looking over the list, he figured there'd be time for 16 songs, possibly more, a handful of which would be band originals.

The audience, most of the time, wouldn't know the covers from the originals. Most of the material played from other composers was obscure and eclectic, not found on top 40 radio and not occupying lofty positions on the charts. Even the familiar songs they played were 'Eclectibleized,' arranged to both honor the original while applying subtle tweaks to the arrangement.

Despite the intended variety of the program, one constant would remain. It would be psychedelic, music for the mind and the soul. Abbas wanted to transport the audience. Solo breaks and improvisation would be encouraged.

Faith and Daniela were sitting in the front room just yards away, sorting vocal duties for the show. Faith would be an on again, off again participant. Splinter was still growing inside her, and getting more lively by the day. She was as excited as the rest of the group though, and would perform as much as possible.

Dani had already parlayed with the boys at the last practice session. Mike sang well, Paul and Geoff, good enough. They all had improved over the years at harmonizing, important for keeping the audience engaged. Some nervous energy was building, she needed to get her groove on, and belt out a few lines.

Robin came skipping down the stairs, happy at the fact that she'd gotten Gabe to take a nap, like his buddy Jake, two doors down. All of Greenbank would be in attendance tonight; the youngest were to sit side stage, or in a loge box with Neff, Aleah, and Hassan. If they got sleepy or fussy there were backstage dressing rooms to crash out in.

Down at the Phil, Geoff and Paul were hauling their rigs out onto the stage. Mike and George were already in place, setting up their equipment while John and Angus were huddled with the venue's tech guys.

John Price was the top local light show wizard, having cut his teeth with the Twenty Third Turnoff, Liverpool's '60s tripping troubadours. Angus Rigby was the Cavern Club's veteran sound man. Both had been here in the past and dreamt of applying their skills in this magnificent hall. The results of their efforts would greatly enhance the evening's festivities.

A collective "Lucas!" welcomed the manager as he strode on stage, eyeing the preparations taking place all around him. "Where's the rest?" asked Paul.

"Obs and Robs are getting them all settled backstage. You guys okay?"

"Fantastic!" said Geoff. "We're nearly set."

"I've got a takeaway laid out in the back, courtesy of Kevin's chippy."

"Another reason you're the gaffer!" Mike said, surrounded by keyboards.

"What's the word, Georgie?"

"Chilled but charged, Luke."

"Cool." Luke liked the vibe; these guys were pumped.

Finding George Pearson had proven to be serendipitous; his optimism and good cheer was infectious. Somehow, despite a resume limited to garages and pubs, he'd become one hell of a drummer, with an amazingly deft touch. Geoff, Mike, and Paul, all of whom had toured with successful acts, were impressed to the point of being inspired by the new guy's chops.

Abbas and Robin were at home here, and could navigate the halls and warrens of the complex blindfolded. They had commandeered a large room for everyone to meet, eat, and stash their stuff, as well as two smaller ones for a changing station and a quiet room. Everyone, including the band, gathered one hour before curtain, just as the front doors opened to the public.

"This is a good-looking bunch," Lucas began, taking a silent head count. "Whoa, you brought the dogs?"

"They looked freaked out Luke," Cyril reported.

"I can't remember a time when they were left completely alone," Ben reasoned.

"All right, keep a low profile."

"We'll get them outside a couple of times."

"Good idea. Okay, you know you can sit side stage or anywhere in the loge boxes that's not occupied by our VIPs. Also, management here would prefer everyone stay seated. I told them good luck with that. They've seen it before. Safety first, nobody gets too rowdy. Questions?"

"I have a comment," Geoff said. "Everyone's seen how much effort you've given to put this gig on, Mister Manager. You're aces, mate, and we're still willing to rename the band St. Luke's Disciples."

Lucas grinned. "Hey, I just do it for the free ticket. Besides, I've never seen a band with a more appropriate name. The Eclectibles is spot on."

"Hear! Hear!"

"All righty then. Let's the rest of us get out of here, let the players summon their mojo."

The hall was filling up nicely, the sold-out crowd anxious. Luke spotted the Moores and Carters, the Everton execs, sitting in the loge, along with Mick and Judith. Neff had brought his potter friend Julia; they were in a box with Roisin and the Mason brothers. There was a buzz about the place, an air of anticipation.

The house lights went down as the curtain opened, leading to some gasps and quite a few oohs and aahs as Aleah's vision of art in stage design was revealed.

John's projection screen was rear stage center, flanked by two huge tapestries, rack mounted, providing a backdrop for the band's equipment. One tapestry was a Persian scene depicting paradise, with figures engaged in the hunt, at a feast, wrestling, and in contemplation, sitting around a hookah under a pistachio tree. The other, borrowed from the Stillwell's, featured the English countryside, with brook, dale, and meadow, alive with creatures of the wood.

The rest of the stage was a swath of color and texture. Strips of material, multi-hued and richly patterned, hung from the mic stands, and were draped across the front monitors. Both percussion stands were festooned with ribbons, and the area between the mics and the amps and speakers, Obs and Robs' playground, was lined with Persian carpets.

And there were lava lamps, nine of them, spread out on the tops of the amps and the backless stools used for holding water bottles and pints.

Suddenly, the only illumination in the hall was those lamps as the rest of the house lights were snuffed and the band took the stage to a spirited welcome.

Facing the audience, they took up their positions. Paul, in an embroidered, western, snap-button shirt, went to the front left mic and strapped on his big, blonde Rickenbacker, followed by Faith and Dani at the two center mics, Dani in an ivy print tunic and a pair of paisley palazzo pants, along with a jemi cap borrowed from Aleah.

Geoff took to the front right stand, his smile the most noticeable thing he had on, acknowledging the crowd.

George was behind him, tucking into his kit, a massive concoction of primal, aural force. Mike was cross stage, amidst his assemblage of keyboards, adjusting knobs and dials.

From backstage center, right between Mike and George, Robin and Abbas strode forward to a heightened round of welcoming applause, joining their mates up front to say hello. Abbas was sporting a kufi skull cap, richly adorned, covering his still scruffy pate.

"Good evening everyone. It's great to be with you again. Nice digs, eh? We're anxious to share our music with you. First, I'd like to introduce our newest member, ladies and gentlemen, the bongo buddha, George Pearson!"

George stepped out and gave a nod and a wave, tossing both sticks into the crowd.

"C'mon Georgie, get us cranked up!"

Now he picked up two mallets, instead of a pair of sticks, and gave a sharp whistle.

Jake and Gabe came running from stage left, grabbed the mallets, and took their positions, each beside one of the two gongs.

"Whenever you're ready, lads."

They both reared back and let it rip, returned the mallets, and ran off stage. Lots of 'aawws' were heard.

Before the resonance died completely, Mike started an introductory melody on the Farfisa organ, heralding the ominous feel of the opener's dark lyrics, Faith issuing the warning:

Poisonous gardens, lethal and sweet

Venomous blossoms, choleric fruit deadly to eat

Violet nightshades, innocent bloom

Omnivorous orchids, cautiously wait, hungrily loom

Then it was on: the crash of a cymbal, followed by bass, violin, and guitar, all at once, driven by George's insistent snare, fast and steady, leading into the chorus:

You will find them in her eyes, in her eyes

You will find them in her eyes, in her eyes

Two more verse/chorus cycles ensued, Faith's pleas to resist the siren's call. The song ended with a crash and fade.

Immediately Mike was back on the Farfisa, another invitation to danger, albeit a bit more melodic. Geoff and George joined, setting the structure, accented by Paul's very fuzzy riff, repeated until Dani stepped to the mic. The song's arrangement called for the chorus before the first verse:

I think it's over now, I think it's ending

I think it's over now, I think it's ending

Bass and drums changed tempo slightly at the verse, George adding more pace:

There is sometimes a later secondary phase

It's not unusual for it to last for days

And everything is magnified when it's gone

The song's only bridge came after the first verse, followed by a word to the wise:

Reality is only temporary
Reality is only temporary

Three more verse/chorus volleys followed, detailing Dani's efforts to aid the listener's return to safe harbor.

Both songs, 'The Garden of Earthly Delights,' and 'Coming Down,' were by the United States of America. The sound was a kind of post beatnik, intellectual bohemia. Lounge psych, if you will. The crowd ate it up. Some were already up and at it.

They were halfway through their first 'mini-symphony.'

Geoff kicked off 'It's Love' with a midtempo bass line, accompanied by George's hi-hat and a brush on the snare. Mike's piano ushered in the first flute break, Abbas setting the mood for the Rascal's soul-psyched jazzy romp. Faith's lilt was evident in the lyrics, delivered with a hop and a skip:

Oh what a crazy feeling, you got my heart reeling
They say it's the weather, but I know much better

Longer and livelier was the second flute solo, amidst some do dos and da das and a couple of wop wops. The last verse heard Faith committing fully to love's pull, Abbas closing out the tune with another break.

A much bigger and fuller sound followed Robin's intro to 'Desiree,' the Left Banke's ode to an elusive 'It Girl.' The New York baroque pop outfit had scored bigger hits with 'Walkaway Renee' and 'Pretty Ballerina,' but Abbas liked 'Desiree's' dynamism. Mike sang lead, with the girls adding opposing lyrics near the end of each verse, and a whole lot of la la las, which served as the chorus. Between each section the whole band played an anthemic four bar set of notes simultaneously, to great effect. Their fade out at the end was replaced by raucous applause.

Mike Pinder's mellotron was featured on 'Desiree,' Ben was thinking it was one of the coolest instruments ever devised.

Developed in his hometown of Birmingham, it was both electrical and mechanical, keyboard controlled. Its case was stocked with pre-recorded tapes, duplicating the sound of whatever was recorded on them. Touch a key and you might hear a cello, or a bugle. Mike actually worked for the early developers of the instrument for a year and a half. He bought a used one and employed it on all the Moody Blues albums thereafter. He changed his up, removing all the special effects tapes and replacing them with more strings and horns. The instrument also had voice tapes, duplicating the sounds of an orchestra's chorale. In short, the thing was a semi-portable symphony in a box.

Paul changed guitars for the next mini set, opting for his Martin acoustic, again, blonde in color. Faith headed for the wings, needing to sit for a few. The band, after a musical tour of America's 'head' lands, was bound for the English countryside.

'Arthurian Dream,' words by Penny, music by Abbas, took them back to medieval times, a folky romp, fraught with the challenges of the era. Paul and Robin combined well, with Abbas and Mike filling in around the edges.

'Dream' segued into 'Winter Wine,' a fairly long suite from one of the Canterbury scene's mainstays, Caravan. At first it was just Dani and Paul with the introductory verse, cueing drums, bass, and organ into the lively remainder of the song. Also set in Arthurian legend, the lyrics featured an adventure set among minstrels and castles, with knights, dragons, and fair maidens. Mike performed a compelling organ solo mid tune and closed the piece with some tasty piano.

An earlier Caravan number, simply titled 'Love Song with Flute,' followed. Again, Paul and Dani, inviting the listener into their little tale, this time one of unrequited love. After the second vocal passage the band swept in with their own pacier section, carrying a more retro feel into the rest of the lyrics. That same instrumental section then repeated, and carried through to the end, overlayed by Abbas' soaring flute breaks. It was awesome!

And it carried right on through to a song familiar to a lot of the audience, Traffic's 'Vagabond Virgin.' Mike and Paul sang, Dani grabbed a drumstick and a wooden block, dancing about as the song's title muse, teasing the audience:

Tell me how you want me to be
Then look again and you will see
That I'm still the same love

An acoustic framework, bouncy and bawdy, carried the tune. Chris Wood's flute on the original was bright and ever present, and Abbas saw no reason to change it up.

The band's sound filled the hall in a way that any musician could only dream of, everywhere and all at once. Clear and crisp, the slightest hint of subtle tone was available, each listener wrapped in an individual cocoon of sound.

Unlike the first set that had the crowd dancing, the second set found the audience content to sit and listen to the band play, watch their interaction and be entertained by John Price.

Angus Rigby's work on the sound board is like a referees' on the pitch; the less you notice them the better they are. With John, however, his efforts made the concert a multi-sensory event, they need to be more than noticed.

The first set was all old school light show staples. Soft reds and blues, drifting over the stage while bubbling, pulsing nondescript shapes, protoplasmic in nature, oozed in and out of focus on the projection screen.

For the second set he employed a brighter approach to the stage while showing still shots of rural English landscapes, sort of like a musical travelog. He looked forward to the next batch of sounds; things were going to get primal.

The band was ready to go again. Faith took the stage and was chatting with the people in front when she suddenly had to pause, holding her stomach, and looking to the wings.

"Shea, be a dear and bring me that stool."

He did so, setting it by her mic stand.

"You okay?"

"Yes, luv, I'll be fine. Seamus McTimons, Everton's new star!" she said to the audience, prompting him to flash a sheepish grin and hurry off.

"Whew, the baby's in the mood." That drew some laughter and back and forth with the crowd. She sat and held her belly.

"Ooph, I tell you what, let's let the little one 'kick' things off, forgive the pun." She cupped the mic with both hands and held it to her belly, low, on the right side. After a few seconds the thump and thud the little one produced was plainly audible throughout the hall. It was answered with a few gasps and a lot of ohs and wows.

"I can follow that beat," announced George, who began a rumble on his mid toms, followed by the beginning of a rhythmic melody.

Faith and Dani picked up a shaker and a pair of maracas, respectively, and got with it.

Robin and Abbas added tambourine and castanets. Luke was surprised. Castanets take some skill to get them going, but Robin was rocking.

Mike went over, grabbed a couple of sticks, and started in on the two big floor toms, bringing the rumble and thunder while Paul strapped a djembe on and went beatnik.

Not to be left out, Geoff picked up the mallets and rolled them softly across both gongs, enriching the mood.

This went on for five or six minutes, shifting, evolving, taking on a life of its own, all the while bathed in color, swirling, and ever changing.

George stopped orbiting his kit and took his stool, beginning a segue into something with more structure, cueing his mates.

Mike went to his Hammond B3, Geoff his Fender bass, and Paul traded the djembe for yet another blonde guitar, this time a Fender Strat. The rest stayed drummed up.

Geoff started a bass line, beginning on high and then descending, repeated four times, during which you could hear the Hammond swelling, the drums building, and a simple guitar chord increasing in volume.

Then, all together, three chords and the truth, in sync, followed by a drum break, repeated twice, afterward falling into a groove allowing Mike and Paul to solo. The song ended with George's furious finale, the audience urging him on.

'Soul Sacrifice' was the title. It had electrified fans at Woodstock, Mike Shrieve a teenager at the time. Abbas remembered jamming with him and Gregg Rolie in San Francisco.

Another quick drum fill, and 'Incident at Neshabur' was launched, also a Santana tune. The first half was similar to 'Sacrifice,' a dynamic interplay between percussion and the other instrumentation. The second half settled into a slow, instrumental seduction, soothing and tropical, with some nice guitar picking and tinkling of the piano keys.

When the applause died down, Obs and Robs and Dani and Faith tossed their noisemakers to the crowd.

"We'll need some help on this next one!" Paul crunched some bar chords, Mike, Geoff, and George answered, and 'Cuban Bluegrass' had the audience back on their feet.

Ben was very familiar with the *Manassas* album. Stephen Stills had spent time in the Tampa Bay area, attending Plant High School. He had assembled a raft of stellar musicians, and together they stretched genres on their debut double album.

It was two verses; Faith on the first, in English, then Dani on the second, in English and Spanish. The short interlude between the two featured Abbas stepping to the mic and announcing:

"Música Latina es Cuban Bluegrass."

Such a lively number, the crowd was dancing unfettered, a fiesta in Liverpool. Dani was singing about the possibilities:

If I could thank you now, feeling much smoother
If I could just be here, make it much cooler
Dale su alma bien, por la descarga
Nada importa pues, en lo que hagas

The original ended soon after, but Abbas cued everyone to rage on. They took turns soloing, driving the frenzy. The crowd were all clapping and cheering, full of mirth and merry.

Abbas had always put a lot of thought into working up a set list. It was something that he enjoyed, and he thought it made a real difference, like the way a band would sequence an album.

It was all about the flow of music. He'd come up with the concept of a four mini set program to mimic the four-movement structure of a classical symphony. The music in the first three sections fit well together. He'd even cheekily named them, a play on terms typical in classical music. The first he called Retro, followed by Domestico and Percusso. One movement remained, Psychedelico. Inwardly he smiled; maybe this ought to remain private.

Faith took a break. It was amazing how active she'd been during the last half hour, and she was surprisingly graceful, dancing about while lugging Splinter around the stage.

Paul changed guitars again, 'different horses for different courses,' as they say. A Gibson Les Paul was just the ticket. And yes, it was blonde.

They were all in place, ready for the nod. Paul hesitated, and looked around at his mates, "Let's bring it home!"

"Yeah!" was the low shout from George, which was the cue for the band to simultaneously begin 'Fresh Garbage,' the opener from Spirit's debut. Clever melodies and a cheeky set of lyrics, reminding the listener to be conscious of Mother Earth:

Look beneath your lid some morning
See those things you didn't quite consume

Dani did the honors, yielding to Faith, who sang the next song from the same album, changing the name of the title subject, 'Uncle Jack':

Have you seen my Uncle Neff
Have you seen my Uncle Neff
Wonder what you're all about
He can bring the inside out

Both songs had a lot of bombast and paired well together. A really unique sound, typical of the variety of material that came out of California in the heady '60s.

Another west coast collective, Jefferson Airplane, was covered next. 'DCBA-25' was the name of the song; what that meant no one had any idea. It was one of their favorites, though, great instrumentation and three-part harmonies:

Too many days I've left unstoned, if you don't mind happiness
Purple pleasure fields in the sun, ah don't you know I'm running
home

Paul Kantner had written an emotional song about relationships in a group dynamic, a song with sadness and hope, and making memories together. Imagine that:

I take great peace in your sitting there
Searching for myself, I find a place there
I see the people of the world
Where they are and what they could be
I can but dance behind your smile

The audience rose as one, much appreciative and feeling that communal vibe. As they settled, the stage darkened except for a spotlight on Geoff. He started a three-note riff, repeating it four times on different octaves, very softly. The spot started to pulse, keeping time with the notes.

There grew a murmur within the crowd. Anyone that had ever seen a big Eclectibles show knew what was coming. Robin was going to burn the place down.

Every sixteen bars, that was the mantra, and the point at which the music shifted, ever so slightly, and became more insistent, gaining its form and gathering its power. 'Catch and Release,' a band original.

George and Geoff were lockstep now, the drummer keeping pace with a muted hi-hat, a second spot illuminating the partnership.

Sixteen bars, a third spot, Mike setting an ominous mood, his mellotron breathing purpose and intent.

Sixteen bars, a bit louder, a bit more urgent, a fourth spot on Robin, emerging from the wings. Her violin was issuing a low groan as she drifted to center stage. A plaintive moan, luring the listener in.

Sixteen bars, stronger now, pacy, Robin adding some arpeggios, more melodic. She glided around the stage, building her solo, enticing the crowd, her three bandmates the only tether to reality.

Sixteen bars, and the tether snapped as Abbas and Paul joined in, reinforcing the groove now reaching fever pitch, the light no longer white and pulsing, but throbbing red, animated by a bank of strobes casting bizarre images of staccato movement.

Sixteen bars, Robin's violin was soaring. All that time spent in the discipline of a classical symphony, with its rules and structure, were now channeled into freedom of expression. She was perched on one of the monitors, at the very edge of the stage, an impossible litany of notes mesmerizing her listeners.

Sixteen bars, and a rip up the scales. As she stroked the highest note, she leapt off the monitor, landing on the stage as the whole band went silent. Four beats later they erupted anew, one long cacophonous din, punctuated by a double gong.

Their sonic assault on the audience was returned in kind, minutes of cheering, shouting, and applause. The band were catching their breath, and beaming at the crowd's energy and appreciation. They all walked around the stage, waving, and taking their bows. It was funny, Dani imagining someone in the crowd thinking to themselves, 'Hey, isn't that my vet?' or 'That's the lady that fills my prescriptions!' There were plenty of familiar faces.

Geoff introduced everyone, summing monikers like The Chairman of the Boards, the Persian Pied Piper, The Axeman, The Devil that went down to Georgia, and the Baking Buddha. John and Angus were marched out and feted, and the audience was asked if they'd like to have a nightcap.

"We'll need some help on this one. Ladies and gentlemen, you haven't' seen him in years, but please welcome back the prodigal son, Mister Ian McTimons!"

What followed was an eight-minute celebration, like an old-fashioned house party! 'Gimme Some Lovin,' a real oldie originally recorded by a teenage Steve Winwood and the Spencer Davis Group.

Psychedelic soul, everyone on their feet. Nearly all the gang in the wings went down to boogie.

Abbas was grinning from ear to ear. Retro, Domestico, Percusso, and Psychedelico indeed!

CHAPTER 52
FRIDAY, 14 DECEMBER

And with the mossy sod first covered o'er,
and taught this aged tree
With its dark arms to form a circling bower

Ben sat under the yew, alone with his thoughts. There were two and a half weeks left in the '70s, cause for reflection. It had been quite the year. Events both planned and those that surprised had availed themselves with regularity. How they were dealt with would always frame the narrative.

Neff had a quote he was fond of: 'once is happenstance, twice is coincidence, thrice is significance.' Here was the key, in Ben's opinion, to the manner in which the Greenbank gang lived their lives. Together. And not just now and then, or most of the time, or as a rule. Always. From the tragedy and terror of the Iranian revolution, to the joy and celebration of the Eclectibles concert, and everything in between. They faced it together.

His theory was supported by a timeline, along which numerous examples could be cited. Luke's trip to Iran to secure safe passage for

Hassan and Aleah. The Mason's purchase of a pharmacy. Cyril's tute-lage of Shea at Everton. The Pines 'adoption' of Cye. The gang's 'adop-tion' of April. Ardavan Concepts and Design. Kevin and Cheryl's trip to Trinidad. The Hajj. Otter and Barky's unflagging vigilance and loyalty. And don't forget the Fixer, constantly at work behind the scenes.

It was a tribe he was very thankful to be a part of. Bring on the '80s.

He had a folder with him, on the folding chair next to his, set against the base of the yew facing west towards the lake. It contained a photograph, and the last chapter of his book. His self-imposed deadline of the end of the year had been met. It needed to be edited and published. That would take months, but it was a nice sense of accom-plishment to be holding a completed manuscript.

He studied the enlargement, taken from the open attic dormer in his own home, a photograph of the very tree he was sitting under. Shot during winter in the late afternoon, the scene revealed a sunset sky, bathing the lake and meadow in its glow. Due to his lofty vantage point, Ben had been eye level with the bulk of the tree's canopy, and the setting sun's illumination.

A flurry of starlings was busy amongst the branches, some silhouet-ted, some visible, some obscured. Though in a way stark and lonely, it was gorgeous, Mother Nature on full display.

He had wondered if it might raise a few eyebrows, putting himself in the book. In the end he decided that making it the last chapter would be a nice touch; he could share with readers his iconic local spot, with its beauty and inspirational power. Then he wouldn't be concerned with the typical and sometimes cheesy author's notes and bio.

Setting aside the print, he picked up the text for one last perusal.

Missives from Merseyside
The Greenbank Yew

I don't suppose that anyone would consider the big tree near my home a local landmark. No one's heard of 'The Greenbank Yew.' Passersby would certainly notice it, standing picturesque in a small field with a lake in the background, and probably pause to admire the scene. It's old, hundreds of years, and beautifully shaped, with a full rounded canopy. But it is a fairly common scene, found in numerous leafy locales away from the City Centre.

Benjamin Pine here. In the course of putting this book together I've learned of what some of my fellow Liverpudians consider the most iconic of places whose image conjures up their love for the city. Their responses have been varied and wondrous, making me all the more fascinated with my adopted home.

I came here from America a little more than 10 years ago with a suitcase, a camera, and a notepad, my friends and I hoping to find a start to our futures. We found a foothold in a rowhouse in Mossley Hill, right across the street from the most awesome tree, which we learned was a yew.

My pal Abbas, who's from the middle east, was familiar with yews, called sorkhdar in his country. Taxus Baccata is the official Latin name of the species, found in Europe mostly, but also in pockets elsewhere. It's an evergreen, with red berries containing its seeds.

It's considered to be the hardest of the softwoods, akin to cedar or pine. Yew wood also has a good degree of elasticity, historically being a good source for longbows. It's also used for making musical instruments and furniture.

Abbas and I used to climb it fairly regularly, until we were alerted to its toxicity. Apparently, every part of the tree is poisonous, save the fleshy part of the berry between the aril, or skin, and the seed. Now we keep the area under the tree clear of any droppings, so the dogs and children don't accidentally ingest any.

The yew is a joy in any season, framed by glare or gloom, and touched by mist and frost. It's also a constant in my life, dominating the view every time I enter or exit the house, or even look out the window.

It's a meeting place, and a start and end point for shared activities. It's hosted garden parties and athletic events, and sometimes it's just the place for a bit of quiet contemplation.

One day my friend Lucas and I were sitting there, and he made an interesting analogy. He spoke of the seeds of the yew, nurtured by the tree itself until it was time to spread their influence elsewhere, borne by birds attracted to the berries.

"That's us bro," he said. "Nothing has been more of a symbol of our

lives here than this tree. We nurtured each other here, and our children will learn what this tree can teach them, and venture out, spreading their own influence."

Luke's an idealist, and a romantic, but he was right. Our progeny, seeds of the yew.

Recently something occurred that drove home Luke's theory. I was under the yew, with my dog, Barky. We were just hanging out after a walk around Greenbank Park. My wife, Faith, came out of our front door and stood on the stoop, supported by our friend, Robin. She had an overnight bag and needed to get to the hospital. It was time.

Our daughters, Hope Elayne and Grace Louise Pine, were born late in the afternoon on the last day of November, mother and daughters both healthy and happy.

Now I have Faith, Hope, and Grace. Who could want for more?

The End
June 28, 2022

Life's a long song,
But the tune ends too soon for us all.

***

Ian Anderson

QUOTED LYRIC INDEX

Chapter • Title • Artist

About the Author

Harold Bell is a historical fiction writer whose passion for world history, the arts and the outdoors is at the forefront of his work. Growing up as an only child, he took advantage of a father whose career was tied to the construction industry and a mother who supported a life of travel. His first 17 years were spent in a handful of states, as well as the Caribbean, Middle East and South America, never living in one place for more than three years. This immersion into widely varied cultures provided ideas for the subjects of his writings.

Harold's love for music has always been a consistent part of his life since the age of ten. His stories feature the songs he grew up with, from the early rock and roll of the '60s through the new millennium. His love for football (soccer), also a theme in his works, began in his early adult life, and for over 25 years he played with local leagues in both the Tampa Bay area and in Colorado Springs.

Upon retirement, a 30-year dream was realized when Harold completed his first novel, Under the Yew, a story of friendship and family set in the late '60s about a group of multi-cultural young people who emigrate to Liverpool in the hopes of creating a life together. Seeds of the Yew picks up the tale some years later, with the Greenbank Gang embracing and confronting events, both in and out of their control, but always together.

Harold lives with his wife of 45 years in St. Petersburg, Florida, along with the best dog ever.

9 781964 239033